The Portal

A Story about Love, Immortality

and the Philosopher's Stone

A Novel by

Russell Burton House

THE PORTAL

This book is a work of fiction. With the exception of historic facts, events,
places and persons, all names, places, characters, corporations, institutions,
organizations and incidents are entirely imaginary; any resemblance to
actual events or to persons, living or dead, is coincidental.

First edition, 2007

Back cover photographer: Russell Burton House

Printed in the United States of America

Published by Triad Publishing, PO Box 116, Winfield, IL 60190 USA
www.triad-publishing.com

ISBN: 978-0-6151-5703-0

For Sue, who asked, *"What happens next?"*

Chapter 1

Say not, 'I have found the truth', but rather, 'I have found a truth'.

- *Kahlil Gibran (1883 – 1931)*

You will find something more in woods than in books. Trees and stones will teach you that which you can never learn from masters.

- *Saint Bernard (1090 - 1153), Epistle*

The man flapped around the fire like an immense crow, his sooty black cloak whipping the dust into boiling clouds. His face was dark with obscene streaks of grime that reflected the seething flames into which he gazed. Streaks of reflected flame in the blackness of his hair made it appear as though a mob of meteors swarmed around his head. The fire was intense, and here he was – a black shadow, a moth that had ventured too close and was in danger of being seared into a stump of carbon.

The haggard crow was now leaning into the blast of flame, his face ruddy and his grimace as intense as though he was preparing to thrust his head into a spewing volcano. Sparks flew off the threadbare sleeves and well-worn gloves as he thrust his pincers into the furnace. Like a swarm of incandescent moths, sparks rose around and above his head and up into the flickering rafters. With a stifled cry, he seized the luminous yellow-orange crucible in the tongs and pulled it forth from the fiery womb like a man attempting to snatch back his tormented heart from a searing Hell.

Dropping to his knees, Richard held out his glowing offering, and then twisted his wrists sharply, adeptly pouring the blazing mass into the iron mold that he had previously heated in the fire and greased with tallow. Silvery liquid fire lunged into the waiting form, followed by increasingly thickening clots, the last of which he shook from the crucible.

Quickly, he began to drum rhythmically on the iron mold with his tongs, as he turned it around with one gloved hand to strike it from all sides. A resonant chime sounded out with each blow. Several times, he shook his fevered head, and a shower of sweat fell, hissing as it vaporized on the hot stones of the floor.

Grunting, he upended the heavy mold, and with a thick metallic thud, a hard plug fell to the floor. This hot ingot was soon in his thick leather mitts. He struck it soundly with a stout iron bar, knocking the largest part of the yellowish crust to the floor. Turning the silvery mass this way and that, every bit of its leprous covering was struck off, revealing a shining mirror of metal. The gloves he wore protected his hands from the heat only enough to prevent a serious burn.

He was exhausted from an evening of work; he had ceased to hear the body's nagging messages some hours ago. Now, the fatigue was too much to ignore. It joined the chorus of aching knees and shoulders, and eyes burning and dry from the heat. He dared not rub them. His forehead was smudged from wiping away sweat with the back of his glove before it washed grime into his eyes. Thirst and hunger pummeled him like spoiled angry twins.

At last, he carried his sacrament to the crude wooden workbench and dropped wearily into the nearby chair.

As he turned the little treasure with his finger, he admired its brilliance, like a tiny toy top of purest silvery metal. Watching the reflected flames as they played on its stellate surface, he puzzled over the Magi, wondering if the star that they had followed had been any more marvelous than the one he now saw before him. Would he ever be allowed to set eyes upon that which he so ardently sought? Was it even possible that this coarse matter could hold so delicate a mystery as he believed? Dozens that he had known, hundreds that he had studied had failed. Could not even the few supposed adepts have lied? The search for the Philosopher's Stone was legendary, and the possibilities that it offered defied the imagination: the ability to transmute lesser metals like tin and lead to the purest gold with only a few grains of the Stone cast into molten metal, and, when used as a medicine, the immediate physical regeneration of the adept, not only curing the most serious diseases, but allegedly assuring physical immortality as well!

Was it even thinkable that 'the Professor' could have knowingly misled him? Perhaps his mentor had become less careful as he had grown older. Perhaps the old man had been deceived.

He longed for rest, and knew that it would not come before dawn began to paint the skies. He settled into the uneasy comfort of those who long for a success that might never come. The philosophical problem, once accepted, cruelly pinned a man through his soul, like a butterfly to the spreading board. Simply stated, Richard understood that he could never say with certainty that any given path in alchemy would or would not yield the Philosopher's Stone – not even those that he and others like him had already worked without success. There could only be the possibility of certainty and exactness when a path met with success.

Even this remote possibility offers a dim hope that quickly fades under examination. Once there is a success in the path of alchemy, once the work is completed in a certain way, under a set of specific conditions, there is no guarantee that the Alchemist has understood precisely the mechanism of Nature that ruled the processes of evolution.

Men once *knew* that the sun rose and set while the Earth stood still in the center of Creation. Their sciences were still able to predict and measure astronomical events with great success, and to explain away the anomalies. There is no satisfaction to be had in doing the impossible if there remains the possibility that a Copernicus can rip the Earth out of the middle of the Universe.

He stared at the furnace and then looked away, realizing that it could not answer the questions raging inside him. He was tired. He understood that in some way his quest approached a spiritual arrogance. It was foolish, perhaps, to try to discover the way of the Adepts, to confect the Philosopher's Stone and become one of the Elect. It was insolent to think that after having done this in one way that it must be done again in yet another way, and perhaps in another still, to be certain that Nature's mechanisms had been truly discovered.

He raised himself unsteadily, the sluggishness of his gate more like that of a man in his eightieth year than one scarcely half that age. He attended to the furnace, preparing it for a period of rest. After the next step, 'marrying Luna with the scaly Dragon', the grosser part of his labor would be done, and that which required strength and intense heat would give way to a period of patience and subtle manipulations. *Dangerous* manipulations, he recalled suddenly.

Still, Richard looked forward to this next phase of the work, realizing that his thoughts and feelings would change along with nature of his labor. The proximity to the fire, the hard labor and concentration that was necessary to prepare the crude matter set into motion a similar cycle of testing and near-torture inside him. It was not unexpected, but it was nonetheless exhausting to confront the ghosts of despair, the thousand voices that urged him to take comfort in an ordinary life, content in the simpler pleasures of family and friends, and to close forever the door to his laboratory and his conceited pursuits.

He knew that this was no longer a possibility, for he had long ago recognized the pattern of his life, had felt the interlocking of his little parcel of being to a larger whole. It had been a simple affair, lasting moments of time, though profound – it had effected a gradual change in every aspect of his life.

With a gloved hand, Richard picked up the crucible from the box of clay, where he had set it to cool after emptying it. He saw that beads of metal had begun to sweat through its bottom. He gripped it hard and it burst into shards on the floor. How fortunate that it waited until now to give up its strength! It had come close to a final fatigue, when it would have spilled its treasure into the ashes to be lost.

As he pushed the pieces into a little pile at the foot of the furnace with his boot, he wondered if his own body would last for as long as it was required. Suddenly, he felt tired and dirty. His stomach gnawed at him, and he needed to bathe – how unworthy it was to think that the sublime intelligence that had fashioned his form would permit it to break in the midst of its usefulness.

Still, he knew that the gnawing pains in his middle were signals that were not to be ignored without danger to his work. Oftentimes he had found himself to be sick and his mind wandering when he did not listen to the body's signals when they first came. When they were ignored, he became increasingly careless, working for tens of hours without food or rest. He had nearly died from the choking acidic fumes from a retort that broke due to his lack of attention. It had taken days of rest and his gentle wife's attention to restore him enough to think clearly, and to take up his work again.

He steadied himself and noted with a start the exhilarating smells of rosemary and lavender. Melissa must have started a bath for him! Now excited, he pushed his head through the door to their room, and was greeted by a generous smile. "I suppose that you are still among the living?" Melissa queried, her voice sweet honey. "Your shadow even looks dirty. Get into the tub and I'll scrub you good".

A scolding like this was a pleasure to receive. Richard recognized that his wife was a true angel. In fact, she had spent years living in a home the center of which was a consuming furnace devouring every spare coin and hour, with a man who devoted himself to reading the words of the long dead, who could not, at times, take notice of the needs of the living. How could one as tender as this, who thrilled in his every smile, be as selfless? He dropped his seared and reeking garments and held his nose in mock disgust as she pushed them back toward the laboratory door.

Melissa sensed that Richard's work was at a new stage – this she could read in his mind. She watched Richard squeeze and contort himself to fit as much of his frame as possible in the hot water. Yes, she was able to read his thoughts like a child reads the fairy writing of frost on the windowpanes. She could see clearly etched there his innermost thoughts and desires – she knew that he loved her and that he was a good man – and yet there was a darkness bordering on despair and eternal loneliness that outlined his gentleness and caused it to stand out in relief. He needed her and she was there for him, as she had been for a long, long time.

Toward noon, Melissa paused in the garden, where she had been gathering herbs. The summery sounds of the twittering birds and the gentle breeze had lulled her into a twilight state, and her hands had been working along, leaving her free to enjoy the passage of images and pleasant memories of other days like this one. The sight of two golden birds chasing along the fence rows had triggered a sense of how special days like this one are. Suddenly she realized that she needed to wake her sleeping companion before their students came!

Pausing briefly in her work, she stood up straight and closed her eyes, mentally traveling to his sleeping figure, and spoke his name, "Richard". She gathered up her skirt, carried her basket into the house, and set it on the table in the center of the room. Richard was sitting up on the side of their bed. He stretched and reached for his shirt. "Missy, I heard you call me".

"You'd better get moving or your students will see their master in bed. Here, make the tea and cut some bread – you are not *my* master. And do try not to make a mess!"

He felt good after his rest, like a man who has escaped a charging bull. His heart beat strongly in his breast as he inhaled the generous smells of a summer day. Quickly he made tea from the fragrant bee balm that Melissa had just gathered. The bread was cut into thick slices and honey and butter were set out on the rude table.

Melissa surveyed the room, and nodded her approval before joining him at the table. "So there isn't a mess to scold me about?" he asked, his head tilted quizzically.

"Don't start with me, Richard, or I'll tell our students how pure your thoughts are when we are alone at night!" They laughed, smiling at each other from behind cups of tea.

"My thoughts *are* quite pure in that they are not adulterated; I am not thinking of anything else!"

They were laughing so hard that they didn't notice that they were not alone until they saw Adam and Mary step into the room and hang their coats on the hooks beside the door. "Do you need a coat on a day like this one?" Melissa asked. "Is it going to get cold later today?"

Adam started to stammer, and Mary said, "We are staying later tonight than usual, as we planned last week".

"We brought fresh meat," Adam blurted out, holding up a large sausage. Richard rose from the table and accepted the proffered gift, passing it to Melissa.

Melissa cleared away the two plates and cups while the others took their places: Mary and Adam on one bench, and Richard on the other. Melissa squeezed along side of her husband, and joined hands with the others. "God of all, God who created all that is by thought, God who lives within our breast and is there revealed, we ask that you will assist us as we strive to comprehend and apply Thy immutable laws. We ask that we may assist in the Great Work on behalf of a suffering humanity. So Mote It Be!"

"So Mote It Be!" all chimed in. They dropped hands and looked at each other around the table.

Mary broke the silence. "We were talking on the walk here about how much we wish that we had been born when you were. What I mean is that we are sorry that we could not be a part of the Order when it was active".

Melissa got up from the table abruptly. "What makes you think that it is not active?"

Adam jumped to his feet. "We... well... We didn't mean it that way. I'm sorry, Melissa".

Richard sat looking at his hands, picking idly at a fresh blister. "We can talk about this if you like," he said quietly. "There is no problem, nothing to regret about your statement. Yes, the Order is withdrawn from view, but it is still vital. There would have been little point in discussing it with you if it were not still a vitalizing channel of the Divine for humanity."

As Melissa and Adam returned uneasily to their seats, he continued. "What we call the Order is in reality an eternal condition, and one can learn, through specialized guidance and devoted exercises, to be in attunement with this condition at any time. That is to say that one can resonate in harmony with this condition or state of being. Melissa knows this as well as anyone, and so she is continually at one with the Order and its work. Perhaps she could better express this to you if she is willing".

Melissa sat upright, closed her eyes, and began to speak in a quiet voice. "The Order was, and is, something that goes beyond its outer form, beyond its visible form. When we were members of a working group, we were aware of its imperfections, of its limitations. In fact, it was as imperfect as any man-made institution could be, despite the high ideals it expressed and the importance of its work. We knew, however, and we knew it with increasing clarity as the time for the Order's departure from the physical world approached, that the real work - that of the *Invisible* Order – was not subject to the flaws of its workers. Certainly we tried to do what we could to express the divine nature of the Work in a material form – this is what all of us do – we attempt to express the Divine in this material realm. Ultimately, this particular vessel of the Order's work became unsuitable for the mission, and therefore the visible work for this particular time came to an end".

Richard appeared to be as spellbound as the young brother and sister, but unlike them, he gazed, not into his wife's eyes, but at the door to his laboratory. "Melissa," he started, "can we start the experiment? The day is slipping away."

"And you preach 'Patience'?" came the response, though with a smile.

"No, it's not a matter of patience; it is a matter of demonstration. I want to show them the doorway. Or at least try."

Mary and Adam looked at each other, each trying to read the expression of the other, and then turned to Richard.

Mary spoke, "You have never mentioned a doorway before, to either of us. What is this door? Why can't you be sure whether or not we will be able to see it – don't you think we are able to paint mental pictures or to see the ones that you and Melissa create for us?" The girl was eager and nearly defiant.

Adam looked bashful, his head down, but his blue eyes danced under his long hair. He was seventeen, almost two years younger than his sister. He shook his head and looked straight at Richard, "No,

Mary, he means seeing something that has existed for a long time – not something that he and Melissa created – and we may not be prepared to see it". All were silent.

Melissa rose, walked to the front door and shut it, and then closed the curtains over each of the small windows. Richard went to the laboratory and returned in a moment with a small brass container and a wooden box, setting it before his wife, and then went again to the laboratory.

Melissa had already lit a candle and placed it in the center of the table. The two young people had moved their bench and adjusted themselves so that they were comfortable, in anticipation of another period of relaxation and mental refreshment. They sat with their backs straight, but at complete ease, breathing gently and evenly. They watched as Melissa gently opened the wooden box and took out a bit of the black powder between her fingers. She sprinkled it carefully into the small brass bowl, which was triangular, much like Richard's precious crucibles. In it was a glowing ember, still radiant from the blazing inferno that had danced in the heart of the furnace less than half a day ago.

The smoke spewed forth wildly, in increasing clouds that dimmed the gentle and shimmering light of the single candle flame. Melissa took yet another pinch, dusted the ember with it, and then closed the box. The smell was hard to describe. It smelled at once fresh, but as ancient as the oldest of trees. It was not like the incense used at church, and yet it was holy. The sweetness was incomparable, and yet it was as heavy as a rain-soaked cloak. It spoke of all of the joyous creativity of untamed nature, and suggested the vast silence of an ancient temple.

Richard returned quietly, so as not to disturb the trio. He had tuned his fragile violin in the laboratory, where it was his constant companion.

The incense! It exhilarated him; he felt the familiar shiver rise up his spine, like a snake uncoiling in the marrow of his bones. He touched Melissa gently on the shoulder, and she nodded, just once, her gaze fixed on the pulsing flame. He saw the liquid pools of light that reflected from the eyes of his students. Their thoughts were already far away as he began to play.

The sinuous tones that he evoked from the strings were those of a land that existed no more. He knew the themes of these compositions intimately, even though neither he nor anyone now alive had heard them performed.

Perhaps they would sound familiar to those who had journeyed among the small villages from the exotic East, or in North Africa. There was richness, a quality of sublime gentleness in the music. As a child Richard had begun to gather to his heart these sounds that he had first heard when he gazed deeply into the night skies or at the shimmer of iridescence on a butterfly's wing.

Only when he became a man in search of God, and had recognized his Path, did this special music begin to develop a pattern, a language. The music was a primeval gateway to a state of consciousness that defied memory, defied rational thought; it could be experienced, but not known.

Melissa listened to the liquid amber sound of the buzzing strings, and heard in the silence behind the music the shades of chanting voices drenched with tenderness. She felt her husband reaching for her, reaching in his mind. They were as one, and they were outside the grasp of time. They saw the stars run liquid in the pale green sky; saw brick-red beaches and brick-red hills cloaked in lavender mists of smoke. A dragonfly with its darning-needle body of shining bottle blue droned in front of their faces, a whirring in the center of their skull keeping pace with it, answering it, a symmetry of sound.

Their lungs were filled with air as sweet as wine, and their intoxication was absolute. Their hearts pounded and the blood poured through every cell, washing up against their insides like waves washing a moonlit shore, pulsing through the tiny stones. Their cells were awash with life! Through each pulsation of the life force they felt the delicate network of fire that vitalized the tiny furnaces in the center of each cell.

Their consciousness was now gathered in their bodies of light, those purified vehicles of their personal consciousness. They experienced the immense power and beauty of the Divine, and they worshipped it, their hearts pouring out blessings, their hearts receiving beyond compare, in one motion of passion. They knew that they *were* the doorway and that they were being summoned.

No one quite knew when the incense sputtered last, or when the violin music adjourned. Richard had risen and opened the curtains. Melissa pinched out the candle flame and smoothed her skirt, stretching her legs under the table. As she bumped the ankles of Mary and Adam, she quickly pulled back, but the brother and sister smiled gently.

"We saw it! Didn't we, Mary?" said Adam.

Placing her clasped hands firmly on the table, examining them intently, the sister answered simply, "Yes."

Having opened the door to the late summer afternoon, Richard walked evenly back to the bench, all of the fatigue from the long night at the furnace erased from his frame. Melissa smiled as her husband took his seat beside her, sensing that he was rested, his body and mind rapidly healing from his immoderate labors at the furnace. He still had the smell of lavender and rosemary from his bath, essential oils he distilled from her garden as a gift for her. It was a gift that she loved to share with him; she knew that this combination helped to restore him physically and mentally when overworked.

The story unfolded quickly enough. Richard and Melissa had waited, neither interrupting, nor prompting, only smiling or making sounds of encouragement from time to time.

Even before the music started, Adam and Mary had begun to feel themselves transported, to feel the seductively familiar quality of the incense, and they permitted themselves to be carried on the wings of the imagination to a land where majestic ancient trees surveyed boundless scenery of green.

Sounds of the exotic music beckoned them, and a fluttering rose up their backs to the crowns of their heads, and they found themselves standing up, their bodies shining like starlight in that silence pregnant with all sounds, in a darkness wherein hid all light.

They knew that they were standing, and yet they felt their bodies to be somehow below them, reclining in a coffin. The sarcophagus was rectangular and fashioned from a single stone, cool and restful.

In velvet skies that stretched out above them, the moon quickly arched toward a point immediately above them. As it approached the zenith, a golden solar disk began to blaze and inched more slowly toward a point just above the moon. In another moment, the sizzling sounds that were rising around them became more mellifluous, flowing together, expressing increasingly lush harmonies.

As Sun and Moon aligned in perfect union, they knew them to be their true father and mother - their Divine parents, whose combined rays glistened upon the cool and dark coffin in the earth. They knew that this was the moment of their true birth - a holy nativity, at once a marriage, a conception, a beginning and a death of all that was before.

Richard recalled the text of the "Emerald Tablet of Hermes": *The father of it is the sun, the mother of it is the moon, the wind carrieth it in its belly, and the earth is the nurse thereof.*

He and Melissa listened apprehensively, as they too had once beheld the mystery of this moment. It had taken many years for them to grasp all that had been revealed, much of which had been merely implied by their teachers and in the ancient writings.

It was all so simple, so pure. They knew that their students had been able to bring back much of their vision for the moment, but could not know how much they would be able to integrate into their daily experience.

"Adam and I saw something else too. This is all so hard to explain. While Adam and I often feel the same way about things, we are not inside each others thoughts in the same way that you and Melissa are."

"Perhaps you are just not aware of where your thoughts are at times, for none of us have thoughts that are purely private, nothing is separate from its source. But go on," Melissa prompted.

"Well, I know that we both felt this moment of birth. Well, you know what I mean. Then the sun and the moon were lined up exactly, and way up above them was a star. It was just a shining point, tiny and silvery."

"What else? What was around you, Adam?" Richard queried.

"It was beautiful, unlike anything I've seen. It was so faint, like it was made out of colored points of light, transparent and glowing, like a fairy castle, it was solid and somehow it shone from the inside. Sort of like the Northern Lights. To the left and right were tall columns, reaching past the level of the moon, with all colors in them, the tops looked like they were painted with blue shapes coming down like the petals of a flower."

"You're right, Adam! I had completely forgotten. Oh! It was so perfect, there was a beam across the top of the pillars, and on it was a disk, with the sun in the middle, like a disk of polished gold, and there were two wings, straight out to its sides, reaching most of the way across the beam. There were lots of stairs, so wide that I couldn't see their sides. But they just went up and up into the temple. It was a temple. I know that! It was a school too, but very old, like it had always been there! I think it was in Egypt". She lapsed into thoughtful silence, her thoughts far away.

"That was the doorway wasn't it? Did we see it? What does it mean?" Adam was forgetting to be shy. "Did you put the picture there for us to see like you sometimes do?"

Melissa turned to Adam. "Did it seem like it came from Richard or me? You are able to know where the impressions coming into your consciousness originate from."

"No. I know how to tell when you are sending pictures. This was like that, but it was more real in a way." Mary had a way of answering for her younger brother. It seemed to satisfy the question for a moment, but then she added, "I don't know where it came from; I've never seen anything like it or heard music like that. What does this have to do with the Order?" Mary could also be demanding and direct.

Richard motioned for Melissa to get a manuscript that was on a low table beside their bed. She spread it out on the floor and they all walked over to look. "Here, this is the coffin." He pointed to the bottom of a complex geometric drawing, rendered in delicate watercolors over black ink. "In the language of Hebrew qabala, it is called *Malkuth*, you can think of it as a level of being, or a world, if you like. Above it is a sphere called *Yesod*." He indicated a violet-colored sphere just above *Malkuth*.

"It has the symbol of the moon, and the one above it has the symbol of the sun," Mary said.

"Yes, these are also the symbols of silver and of gold for alchemists, as you know. That sphere is called

Tiphereth." Richard pointed to a circle painted in a luminous yellow in a line straight above *Yesod*.

"And where is the star?" Adam asked.

"Perhaps it is here, in *Kether*, at the top of the diagram, or perhaps in *Binah*. I will not say for sure what you saw, even though I saw much the same as you did."

"What is this drawing?" Adam quizzed Richard. "Is it old?"

"Its origin is ancient, although I started to make this copy myself some years ago, a little at a time as I could manage to put the pieces together. I copied parts of it from different drawings and am trying to make it more complete still. In our training, some attention was devoted to qabala, it related to the symbolism of our ritual work, and explained much related to the evolving states of consciousness that were truly the objects of our work. Most of this teaching was given orally, and some portions of this diagram might be drawn during a lecture and then quickly erased. Teachers never give us anything for free! We have to work on our own with their assistance."

Melissa pointed to the left and right sides of the diagram. "These are the columns at the left and right, and they relate to the other planetary energies. On the left here are Saturn, Mars and Mercury, and on the right are Jupiter and Venus. Someday, if you are fortunate, you will go up this tree and right through here". With her finger she indicated a winding path up the tree, ending at the blue sphere labeled with the symbol for Jupiter. It also bore the word 'Mercy'. It is only through mercy that you can rise above this level, and at that time more is revealed and you are able to experience higher realms of being. In this regard, think back to the writings of Jakob Böhme or Emmanuel Swedenborg or other mystics that we have shared with you. Böhme, for example had a profound experience while looking at the sunlight reflected from a pewter dish that affected the rest of his life; he felt that the nature of Man and God, good and evil, and the true structure of all creation had been revealed to him in a moment."

"Have you and Richard gone above that level that you referred to as 'mercy', or is this why he is uncertain about the star?" Mary asked, turning toward Melissa.

"Melissa and I have always managed to avoid certain questions that you ask, to avoid stepping into that sticky web. We don't wish to evade your earnest questions, but an answer would not mean anything to you at present. In fact, an inappropriate answer might delay your progress," Richard said evenly.

"I didn't mean to pry, but this is so exciting," Mary chirped.

"No harm done, Mary," was Richard's reply. "You and Adam can ask us anything, and we will answer directly if we know, or admit that we don't know. There are some few things that we might choose not to answer because they will be better answered by your own experience at the proper time."

"Richard, show them that there are no ill feelings," Melissa said with a teasing tone. "Show them your picture".

Richard unrolled another parchment, a small one. He set it down on top of the larger document, and each person reached gingerly to hold down a corner of the picture.

Mary and her brother had gasped. "That is it!" Adam said excitedly.

Melissa smiled at Mary, who was for a moment, quite speechless. Mary regained her speech. "How can we have all seen the same thing so clearly, Melissa? Did you see it too?"

Melissa rose and walked to the open front door, the sounds of her bare feet pounding softly on the polished stone floor blending with the whirring, buzzing and chirping sounds of late afternoon. The sun drove the long bluish shadows of the small house toward the front lawn.

"Yes," she finally spoke, as if to the squirrels dancing up and down the oak tree outside the front door. "I remember seeing it for the first time, during a daydream as a girl. I had sneaked out of the church school on a Sunday morning and had gone to the old cemetery on the hill overlooking the city, and had found my favorite old tree there. It was a special place for me to be alone with my thoughts about God and the church and what life would hold for me as a young woman. I was in turmoil because I loved God and the Bible and all of the wonderful stories, but I was unhappy with the way we were taught, and felt that people should come outside and listen to Nature instead of being inside of a stuffy old church."

The brother and sister had silently made their way to their bench at the table, listening to every word. Richard had let the drawings roll themselves into nice even cylinders on the floor, and had seated himself on the bed, respectfully silent.

"I fell asleep," Melissa continued, "and that is when I found myself in a coffin at the base of the tree. I loved that old oak and felt comfortable wrapped in its thick roots, and knew that I was safe. At the same time, I could see as though I was standing up, in what I now would call my *body of light*, and I saw the tree as a tremendously powerful living being, with a light body similar to mine, as vibrant as the sun itself. The sky was dark, and the sun and moon paused in their courses exactly above me and baptized me with their combined vibrations, they birthed me, and destroyed me, consuming me with fire, purging me, and bathing me in waves of fire.

"When I awoke, I went back to my home, and straightaway to bed. My parents found me and assumed that I had been taken ill that morning. It was fully three days before I ate a full meal, before I could think about school or my chores. My parents worried, but were gentle and loving, and knew that I was going to be well. My mother knew that my body had just started changing into that of a woman, and kept me supplied with teas from the garden and toast and jam.

"I drew a picture in my book, with colored pencils, and wondered what it all meant. I knew that I had been born again in some way, and that I was no longer the same.

"I saw the image again in a temple of the Order. It was during rehearsals for a certain initiation in which I served to tend the flame as the symbolic Colombe, or dove of the temple. In the East of the temple, in preparation for the initiation, was hung a large painting. I was shocked to see that it was *my* tree, *my* tomb, *my* portal to the temple of light, all perfectly represented by a masterful artist!

"It was fortunate that I did not have to act or speak a part for some time, for I was wholly absorbed in examining the painting in every minute detail, and feeling the powerful emotional and physical responses that it evoked.

"The ritual disclosed simply that the candidates by this time in their preparation might be ready for birth onto a higher level, and that at this time they would be inwardly tried and tested to see if they were worthy of entering the Master's temple. They were to be tested by their motives and aspirations, in fact. Of course, there were other symbolic discourses and dramatic events for the candidates, but nothing held my attention in the way that the painting in the East did.

"On the night of the actual initiation, I could not gaze at the painting in the way that the candidates did, because I sat facing them. I scanned their faces, searching ardently for signs of recognition, hoping to find another one who might now be seeing their daydream materialized on canvas."

"Did you find anyone, Melissa?" Mary asked, barely above a whisper.

"Not that night. I was heartbroken. Almost six years later, when I was just over twenty years old, the same initiation was performed. At that time I was presiding over the initiation in a different role. On that night, I laid eyes on Richard for the first time, at least in this life, and he saw the portal for at least the second time."

"It was like I was on fire," Richard declared, resuming his seat at the table. "You cannot imagine the effect. I was twenty-two years of age at the time, and had dedicated my life to the Order and to the study of alchemy. In fact, I had spent most of the three years before that in intense study of these topics as a probationary member of the Order. The Grand Master of the work in our country came to my uncle's home where I then lived, and after the two of them had a brief discussion, I was invited to accompany the Grand Master as his assistant while on an extended business trip.

"I knew that he had a deep interest in all occult matters and that he was a deep student of both qabala and alchemy, but he clearly indicated to me and my uncle that the primary purpose of this trip was business. My uncle knew that I was hesitant to leave my precious books and to stop some of my experiments for the time that the trip was to take, but he suggested that I might learn more from a Grand Master than from any number of books. I was to receive moderate pay, as well as room and board for assisting him in arranging for transportation of antiques and keeping records of his acquisitions.

"During the third week of travel with this gentleman, he suggested that I take a trip on my own to examine one of the enigmatic buildings at a university several hundred miles distant. He gave me enough money to take care of my expenses for the trip, and, along with it, the address of a professor at the university who would find me a sleeping room at the dormitory there. He promised to join me soon. This was going to be quite an adventure!"

"While I had always been a thinker and experimenter, content to live among books and bottles, I was impressed by how easily my employer met with people, how happy he was to see them, and how they lit up around him. He was unlike anyone I had known. He was so patient, and kind. He would talk with the uneducated and the poorer classes of people and they were immediately trusting of him, and didn't feel that he was talking down to them. His listened to beggars as though they were sages.

"Among the aristocrats and intelligentsia, Siegfried was held in the highest esteem. While enthusiastic to try to emulate some of his manners of dealing with people, I thought it best to start with strangers. Taking a short trip would let me begin to try exercising some of these new ideas, and to let me see if it would come naturally and easily, or if it would seem artificial. I agreed at once, and made arrangements for travel.

"The results of that experiment are a whole tale in themselves. In short, I arrived at the university, looked up Professor Koenig and found myself moved into a guest room in his private home. I suspected that he had found me so absolutely charming and wise that he didn't want to have me move into a dormitory room. My host lectured on chemistry, as chance would have it, and he knew Latin, Hebrew, Aramaic, English, Greek, Italian, and a few other languages in addition to his native German. I thought he was Paracelsus! As our visit took place during a break between class sessions, we had few distractions.

"He let me have complete access to his library. My first impression was that it was a rather modest collection. I had been able to collect a few books of my own, you see. The room was not one-fourth as large as this whole room, and it had a huge table in its midst, with three chairs. I had decided not to appear ungracious, and was being generous with my praise when I saw a book by Weidenfeld that stopped me in mid sentence. I had seen some brief excerpts from this author and his writings, and they implied that they were from a larger text. As Weidenfeld was a particularly lucid writer, I had prayed that he had written more.

"Virtually grabbing the book from the shelf, the first of four volumes, I saw that behind this row of books there was yet another row of books! 'Ah, Weidenfeld, so you know of him?' the Professor smiled. I said that I had read only a little portion of his works and had found him clearer than most writers on alchemy. He scurried to the table and began to clear a space, and motioned for me to sit. He took a large stack of books from the chair that he pulled out for me."

Richard continued to tell the tale, letting his memory become completely immersed in fond remembrances from a time long past. "I stood there with the well-worn volume in my hands, in the midst of the old professor's library. He said 'I'm sorry for the chaos; you see, I am in the midst of some inquiry that is leading me though virtually every book in my collection. I fear that every surface gets piled up with books. Once in a while, I spend a day adding a few entries to my index and straightening up afterwards. The index is here, in fact'."

"He then showed me a small book, a catalog of perhaps half of the collection. Over the course of the evening we reviewed his notes together, as excited as two school kids, and in the morning we collapsed on couches in the shaded porch.

"There was no question about it; I had found a mother lode of alchemical books and manuscripts. I puzzled over why the Professor was content to build up a large library, large in the sense that virtually every book was on alchemy, whereas he maintained only a very modest laboratory. When I had asked to look at the lab, the Professor led me to a small corner room that showed signs of only moderate use. There was a broken retort or two, some crucibles with vitrified green-yellow glass erupting through cracks along their sides, and perhaps a dozen sealed vials holding an assortment of oily liquids. I noted the coating of dust that covered it all, and decided that I was in the home of a 'library alchemist' rather than a genuine spagyrist, but I thoroughly liked the man, and realized that his library was a treasure trove."

Richard related his memories to Melissa and the young brother and sister. He apologized for getting so caught up in the details of his reveries, but none of them pressed him to get to the point, so he continued with his tale. He recalled that the next day was spent relaxing in the garden in back of the house, looking through various manuscripts, and drinking spiced lemonade after the delightful lunch. The afternoon had passed quickly.

His employer, Siegfried, had arrived an hour before dinner time, and Richard was genuinely glad to see him. He enjoyed watching how the two men greeted each other warmly, and then over glasses of wine slowly brought each other up to date on what had transpired over the past year.

They had met each other through the Brotherhood, as they called the Order, even though it had admitted women for as long as anyone could remember. At times they had traveled together, studied together and passionately debated conflicting theories of the cosmos. Both had a surprising knowledge of healing; Richard recognized that their learning was beyond that of many practicing physicians.

"Suddenly, Siegfried had said: 'Richard, Professor Koenig tells me you have not been to the university yet, since you have managed to insinuate yourself in the midst of his library. Let us go and examine the building that I mentioned to you'.

"I had then asked 'But won't it be too dark to see much of anything?' and was told 'No, not if we go now.' And so the three of us stepped out into the last light of the day, and walked the four blocks to the main campus of the university. There was almost no activity, as school was not in session. Siegfried asked, 'What do you see, Richard?' indicating the large building in front of us. I explained that 'It is a bit unusual; it seems to have been transported here from another era and set down on this campus. It makes me think of France, and yet I don't know why. The building obviously has eight sides, and has a smattering of gargoyles and other carvings along its top. But wait, here is a dragon! It follows right along the chimney on this side. And, I see a Masonic emblem, the square and compasses over here!'

"I ran along ahead of the older men, trying to see all that I could in the gathering darkness. They caught up with me where I was carefully studying a large carved portal, intricate with symbolic carvings that were indistinct in the twilight. Directly over the door was a dragon, with two small wings, and it was looped into a perfect circle, biting its tail in its fierce teeth.

"I said something to the effect, 'It is obviously an alchemical symbol. My word! Who would decide to decorate a building in this manner?' By now, the Professor had walked right up under the arch, and had raised the heavy brass knocker and had sounded two distinct signals. I started to protest that no one was here, that school was out, when a light suddenly flickered in a stained glass window high above and then just to the right of the door. It became brighter and then slowly faded. Just as it had dimmed completely, we heard two more knocks from inside, then the sound of heavy hinges turning. 'Enter brothers!' came the call from within.

"And so I was brought for initiation, after almost exactly three years of preliminary study in the outer section of the Brotherhood. I will not disclose exactly what transpired, let it suffice to say that when I saw this painting, this amazing painting in the East of that temple, and when I saw, at the same time the eager face of Melissa searching mine, I was literally transfixed. I could not speak or move.

"Of course, it was that the outer events were fanning into flame certain memories, certain inner tensions and desires, and the rapture was certainly an inner one in that sense, but I was wholly overcome".

Melissa interrupted. "And you didn't appear too shy in seeking me out after the initiation," she teased.

"I had no choice but to talk with you – it was like my whole life was beginning again at that point. We talked for almost two hours," Richard told Mary and Adam, "and when I begged her leave so that I could join with my waiting companions and return home, she merely tucked her arm around the waist of the Professor and asked, 'So you have met Father and been to our home already? I am so sorry that I have been so busy here. We have been busy preparing for the arrival of Brother Siegfried and it has taken all of my time.'

"I nearly fell to the floor, as you can imagine!"

Mary and Adam nodded in agreement with Richard.

"So, what happened then? Did you get married and live happily ever after?" Mary asked Melissa.

"Not yet," Melissa replied to the young sister, "though..." She had turned to face her husband.

Richard smiled, continuing to look deep into her eyes. "It all seems like it just took place, doesn't it Missy?"

"When we returned to the Professor's home, I bore but little resemblance to the young man who was traveling for the first time abroad. I felt as though I had journeyed over tens of centuries. The ritual was, in itself, carefully designed to assist the neophyte in coming into contact with an eternal part of themselves – to attain to a particular type of consciousness. As I said earlier, one objective of our Order was to assist us in elevating the consciousness in a safe manner so that we might experience something like Böhme and others did. Often the experience was triggered by events during ritual work, but typically the insights came little by little, during the following weeks or months.

Richard continued. "The painting of the 'Master's Temple' to most of the candidates probably appeared merely as an exalted condition to which we were to aspire. Few of them, unless they had spontaneously experienced something of that state of consciousness beforehand, would suspect that it was more real than anything they had ever encountered. It is more real than our normal consciousness, in that it is timeless.

"Like Melissa in the cemetery with her ancient oak, I had encountered a vision of the 'doorway' some years before. This doorway or portal had beckoned to me, had caused me to look for this special school, this Invisible College, as this aspect of the Invisible Order is sometimes called. It was significant that Melissa and I had both encountered this vision, and perhaps we will talk more about this some other day – what is important now is that you too have seen it".

All sat quietly for a time, deep in reflection. Melissa quietly began to cook the sausage with potatoes and peppers from their garden. Soon, the sumptuous bouquet of various spices mingled with the last lingering traces of the incense and the faint and peculiar smell of the laboratory to which all had become accustomed.

"So, where did you learn more about alchemy, since the Professor could not help you?" Adam asked?

"Well, he was able to help me, after all, Adam, although he was the first of several initiators in alchemical practice. Professor Koenig asked if I would consider staying a bit longer since I had such a deep interest in alchemical practice. After I agreed that this would interest me – in fact it was my dearest desire – Siegfried revealed that the real reason for having me accompany him was to provide an opportunity for me to be initiated, and to put me into contact with the Professor, who was, at this time, responsible for alchemical research and teaching within the Order. Siegfried explained that he had taken my uncle into his confidence before we left for the trip, and had indicated that such an offer might be made to me for further study, if I was found to be ready.

"So, I was found to be ready! And I was going to be permitted to stay here near the Professor, my beloved books, and with dear Melissa, with whom I would now take a walk every afternoon. She and I talked about everything imaginable! We talked about our own experiences in finding the portal and how this had shaped our lives from that point forward. She had been a member of the so-called Inner Order for several years now, and I had just entered it. I had so much to ask her; she was close to my age and was very candid about what membership in the Order entailed.

"Still, I was unconvinced that the Professor could teach me the practical aspects of alchemy. I was certain that he was a chemist, but this was not the same thing. Some have remarked that chemists see matter as dead, whereas alchemists recognize and work with the life and consciousness inherent in matter by virture of its origin in the Divine. Certainly he must have been a competent chemistry instructor or the university would not keep him on, unless perhaps his tenure obligated them.

"The Professor and I walked to the university after breakfast the next morning, and I examined the lecture hall and the laboratory proper. Both were certainly well equipped, and were spacious and well lighted. In the lab, I noted the usual charts on the walls, and one mildly interesting engraving of some anonymous 'puffer' at work in a cluttered medieval laboratory. Still, there was nothing even moderately indicated that there was anything taught beyond basic chemistry. This held little interest for me. I was more than a little disappointed, and I fear that my host knew it.

"That evening, he suggested that we go to his laboratory to 'look around a bit'. Having already closely examined his dusty workshop in the corner of the library, but fearing that I might offend this gracious man, I followed him. He took me by the arm and steered me right past the small room to a closet door just past it. Then, carefully, he swung the door open, and motioned me into the revealed room.

"It was amazing. I had never suspected that the house was so large. While it was not a very large room, it was very efficiently organized. It was full of glassware, and the obligatory furnace was in the far corner, surrounded by boxes bulging with crucibles and a low table by it was surrounded with various mixtures. There was a wall lined with glassware, some of it modern in design, and some of it obviously fashioned after old designs, long considered obsolete. This was not the laboratory of a chemist!

"We looked around for almost an hour, and examined various bottles that contained the results of experiments in alchemy. Once again, he took my arm, and guided me up the rude wooden steps at the back of the room. At the top he coaxed, 'Go on in', and I pushed back the curtains that closed off the upstairs room."

Melissa's voice chimed as clear as a bell. "Time for dinner. Let's get the table cleared off. Here, Mary, you and Adam help me with these dishes, please."

"Not now, Melissa," cried Mary.

"Yes, now," came the reply. "We need to eat while the food is warm".

Chapter 2

Teachers open the door. You enter by yourself.
- Chinese Proverb

Mary and Adam always treasured dinner at the home of their teachers. The food was simple, but never bland. Melissa used various spices from the garden to inspire even the most insipid of foods and to coax from them delicate flavors. From soup to cookies, every part of the meal owed its unique savor to some fragrant leaf, root, or seed that had come from her lovingly tended garden.

Melissa had adopted every sort of medicinal and culinary plant that would grow on their property. Richard was able, from time to time, to surprise her with a cutting or seeds from some truly exotic flora. Their associates who traveled kept an eye out for opportunities to bring some rare or unusual specimen to their friends. Mostly, though, it was Melissa who had found the various herbs, shrubs and trees, while on her long hikes across the fields and wooded areas surrounding their land.

Even though she had been fond of plants as a child, and had let her study mature, even as she had matured, Richard was full of admiration for her seemingly endless wealth of lore and practical knowledge of medicinal plants. Tonight, however, it was her mastery over the delicate blending of the various piquant qualities of plants, and not their use as healing agents that attracted comments of admiration.

It was only after all had sampled every dish, and had honored their hostess with the highest of praise, that anyone thought to ask Richard about what he had discovered beyond the doorway at the top of the stairs.

Just as Adam had begun to remember where the story had left off, his taste buds staggered by a dessert of wine marinated pears spiced with ginger and orange rind, Melissa had prompted, "Well, Richard, aren't you going to tell them about Daddy's attic?"

Smiling, she sat back watching her husband intently, ready to relive the first days of their love and their discovery of each other. Yes, she remembered the laboratory, too. She recalled how her father would go to bed exhausted, his mind too full of abstractions to sleep, and soon he would be in his library, where she would find him in the morning, asleep with his beloved books. She had worried about him, and yet she knew that it was he who belonged to alchemy, and not the other way around. "Alchemy is like a jealous mistress," her father would tell her, "and those who try to deviate from her narrow pathway will soon fade away". And now her husband was an apostle of alchemy, and she found life with him as natural as breathing.

"Well, where were we? Oh yes, I had finally been permitted to see the laboratory of my mentor, and had found it to be as efficient and well-equipped as I had hoped. What more could there be? What greeted my eyes was beyond my comprehension at that time. It was his private laboratory, and what a laboratory it was! The room was essentially half of the upper story of their home, and this rude stairway that we had used was the 'back entrance', the primary entrance being a doorway from his upstairs bedroom to the lab.

"The smaller laboratory we had just left was his teaching lab, for students of the Order who came from time to time to meet with him to carry out the requirements for their studies. Examination showed that there was a block and tackle fixed to a beam that extended from the top of his house so that he could haul supplies into the laboratory from the grounds below through a pair of sliding doors.

"The Professor showed me some of the various experiments that he was working on. For example, he had prepared the oils of gold, silver, antimony, carbon, copper and iron. There were the results of investigations of all sorts, into solvents prepared from tartar, as well as from urine and from sulphur, and works with various mixtures with antimony to animate metallic mercury such as Isaac Newton had done. He seemed to have worked with all of the major alchemical paths I had read about.

"He indicated with a wave of his hand a long table which was littered with notes and a clutter of apparatus. An exhaust port covered the upper part of the distilling tower, and a fan carried the fumes outside. This was obviously where he was spending most of his time. The bright beams of the full moon from the skylight reflected off of what appeared to be a large box of mirrors.

"Taking a piece from the box, he dropped the heavy shiny button of metal into my hand, saying, 'This is the so-called starry regulus of antimony'. He indicated that I should keep it. I had never seen one before, had never had a furnace hot enough to work with it, or even a source of the ore. I was suitably impressed to see a large box full of these. I inquired if he was making the 'fire stone' of Basil Valentine, and he replied that he was not following Valentine in this case, but rather Flamel."

"Flamel! He and his wife made the Philosopher's Stone!" cried Adam.

"Was that what your father was doing?" Mary asked Melissa, her eyes dancing.

"Yes, he was," Melissa replied.

Melissa went on to explain, "It is true that Nicholas and Perenelle were adepts. It is often written that they were members of the Order although such things are easily claimed. They did succeed in making transmutations, and endowed various churches and hospitals and built several chapels in France. This was in the 14th Century.

"My father had long studied alchemy before he came across sufficient texts to assemble a theory on how the Flamel's had proceeded. When he came up with a workable model, he began staying at the lab for increasing numbers of hours, and didn't take the time to see but the closest of friends. He did continue to see his students, and had them working hard in the lab, producing antimony regulus, although they did not know what he was working on himself. Perhaps they suspected that he wanted them to become more skilled at working with the fire, and they were glad for his expert guidance."

"Did he ever succeed?" Mary asked.

Richard responded quickly. "We shall talk about that later, perhaps, Mary. Do not push on this, I ask you please," He was very clearly serious about this, and in fact was uncharacteristically solemn in his manner.

Melissa got up and began fussing with dishes, humming to herself quietly. Her humming seemed mindless, as though it was to assure some privacy rather than to express a song of joy.

Richard continued, "We exited through his bedroom on our way downstairs that evening. It was small, but looked quite comfortable. We paused but for a moment, but I noted the Eastern influences in the decor. There were paisley printed pillows on the bed, which was in turn draped with a wispy fabric screening that would have looked more at home in the tropics than in Europe. Stone and brass statuettes, and incense burners, some appearing to be quite old, were displayed in a corner cabinet, and the walls were a dark green, with dark wood paneling and trim. There was a fragrance of rich, balsamic woods and of old roses, rich with perfume.

"There were less than a half dozen books evident, which made this room an exception to the rule. A painted wooden symbol of the Rosy Cross with distinct hermetic symbolism around it laid flat on the top of the low table and beside it a menacing looking dagger that was now relegated to the domestic task of opening correspondence. It looked as though some genii had set it down while passing through.

"I did see that he was working on a diagram of the 'tree of life' – the symbol that I showed you earlier with the colored spheres. It showed the tree as though it was the inside of the Temple, and as though the temple was the body of Man.

"He took me to the kitchen and set me down at the table and asked Melissa to 'see to our guest' so that he could retire for the evening.

"That evening was like some magical treasure that continually expands and unfolds with new splendor before the eyes! My library alchemist had been transformed into some mythical being that was pursuing the Stone of the Wise beneath the very roof that I slept under at night, and he had placed this totally dazed young man into the hands of his lovely daughter. I didn't know whether to laugh or cry!"

Everyone laughed and Melissa sat wiping tears from her eyes, beaming. "You were surely a sight. I had been hoping for days to get a chance to just sit with you and get more of your attention. At night when you looked through books, I was thinking of this fine young man who was already too old beyond his years, almost too serious. You seemed rather shy around me."

"I wasn't particularly shy that evening," came the carefully measured response.

"And neither was I," she replied.

"The next morning, I could scarcely wait for Siegfried to rise so that I could thank him for his part in arranging for me to study alchemy," explained Richard. "He left before dinner, but not before assuring me that my uncle would be glad for my choice. He presented me with a fair amount of cash, saying that these were my remaining wages for helping him, and indicating that I should be able to pay my expenses as a student, and to help with expenses for my meals, as well as to pay for fare back home when the time came. I was not to be charged for the teaching itself, but rather for materials and equipment that I would use.

"And so, I came to live with an alchemist and my future wife," he concluded. "I know that we have previously been somewhat guarded about our personal lives with you, because the details of our journey are not what is truly important. It is *your* life that is important. We want, really, to let you know just how wonderful and beautiful the world is, and how it provides all that is necessary, although sometimes through seemingly mysterious means."

"Your story is just wonderful. It is like a fairy tale, and yet it is true. We really love the both of you, and like to be able to share in some of your experiences," Mary spoke joyfully, sipping her fragrant tea. The scent of chamomile, peppermint and rose made for a delicate perfume, and everything was just right.

Adam explained, "Mary and I were never even sure where you met, just that you had both been in the Order. I did not know that your father was an alchemist, too."

"Yes," Melissa said, sipping her tea, "He had been in the Order for more than a decade before I was born, and he raised me by himself, after my mother had passed away when I was seven. My parents had married when Father was nearly fifty, and Mother was only twenty-nine. She had been somewhat delicate, but was beautiful.

"It is time for us to leave, as we will be expected home, so that we can go to church early tomorrow. I do wish we could stay longer, but our parents will worry!" the sister said, getting up and retrieving their coats.

"I didn't think we would need the jackets, Mary. It is still warm outside."

"Shut up, Adam," the older sister said, teasingly.

"Come again next week," Melissa said, hugging each of them in return. They hugged Richard warmly, and left the small home, following the well-worn and familiar trail down to the creek, under the light of the full moon of mid-Summer.

Melissa slipped her arm around Richard's waist and leaned close to him, quietly speaking, "If you aren't going to be in the lab tonight, perhaps we..."

"I was just thinking the same thing, Missy".

Richard arose early that morning, and had a light breakfast with Melissa, and then they bathed. He had bathed first, because he wanted to start to work at once, but he stayed to wash her back, and to rub some scented oils into her long hair. Her hair was turning light from the summer sun, and it fell in soft curls past her shoulders.

His hair was still as black as obsidian, but his beard was showing some signs of gray. He kept his beard cropped short, because his wife liked it that way, but his hair was growing unruly, like a child's. Melissa had promised to cut it when he had time to sit still for her. And so it continued to grow.

He made his way to the lab, dressed not in his long coat, but in a dark pair of plain trousers with suspenders, and a long-sleeved white linen shirt. He had found them set out for him beside the bed and rather than look for something else, he had put them on. He had rolled up the sleeves to the crook of his elbows, for even though the dirtiest part of his work was complete for the present, he didn't want to ruin a good shirt.

Richard started pounding on the round, silvery antimony ingots in the largest mortar he had. It had been a gift from the village pharmacist, whose father had owned it before him. When he had cured the pharmacist's daughter from a dangerous fever, he had made it clear that he could not and would not accept any payment from him. The man had persisted, saying that he would someday return the favor. He had taken the pharmacist into his confidence, only to the extent that he had to, saying merely that he was an amateur chemist, and a preparer of some useful remedies. "This remedy was from an old formula from Basil Valentine," he had said.

"He was an alchemist, Richard! We studied about Valentine; he was the first to record many of the now-known compounds. But, he also claimed to make medicines from antimony, which is a virulent poison. It is seldom used today in any form, because it is so toxic. I don't suppose that you are proposing to give my daughter antimony!" he laughed.

Richard had replied that it was indeed antimony that he offered, however it was no longer poisonous. To prove it, he had gone to the man's table and taken a small glass and poured about twenty drops of the golden-yellow tincture into it, and then added a half-ounce of Cognac and an equal amount of water. "To your health," he said, drinking the glass at once. "If it is poison, then I am a fool. If you want, you can sit here and wait for me to become ill, or you can give your daughter three drops of the tincture mixed in three or four ounces of water."

The pharmacist's eyes were as wide as saucers. "How often do I give it to her?"

"Three times a day, preferably on an empty stomach. I will stay here for the first dose, and come back in time for the next one. She will be fine."

The man had complied at once, and by the time the third dose was given, she had regained her color, the fever had broken, and she slept peacefully. "Continue to give the tincture for the next two days, please. I suggest that you and your wife each take a half-dose — you have not rested, and your vitality is down. It is easier to deflect disease than to cast it out."

"What can I do to thank you, Richard? Here, let me pay you something for your trouble, I cannot thank..."

"I cannot accept any payment; I am merely trying to carry out the work of the Master."

"Oh! Yes, I am a religious man too, but I cannot give any medicines away for free, and still care for my family, Richard. Please, I want to pay you something."

"I must insist in doing things in this way; I am truly pleased for your daughter's recovery, but we must look to God as the source of all healing. The medicine was, in a manner of speaking, a gift of God, and cannot be sold".

"You say that you made it from antimony?"

"Yes, it was from antimony."

"From the mine? I mean from an ore?"

"Yes, from stibnite." said Richard.

"And you made this tincture yourself?"

"Yes."

"Well, I'll be!"

They had parted, and the next morning, Richard had found on his front step an extremely large mortar and pestle of iron, and on it, freshly painted was the ancient symbol for antimony. A note, under the heavy pestle read: *This was my father's and was old when he bought it. It has been on display in my shop for years, and I have never had an occasion to use it to prepare medicines. I want it to serve others and entrust it to you for that purpose.*

Richard had often used it in his work and thought fondly of his benefactor each time that he did so. In fact, it was the pharmacist and his wife who had encouraged their children, Mary and Adam, to seek out the 'chemist and his good wife' who had been, in their father's words, 'the hands of God in our time of need.'

The two children had approached Melissa after church, where she taught Sunday school, and had invited her and Richard to dinner the following Sunday. Melissa graciously accepted, and so they shared a wonderful meal with the pharmacist and his family. After dinner, the children were asked to change clothes so they could go for a walk together.

The pharmacist explained that their children were intensely curious about nature, about so many things that he and his wife knew but little. "Yes, I have a degree in pharmacy, but my education was quite focused and perhaps too narrow in scope. I regret that I had little exposure to what was once taught as 'natural philosophy', which I think was a more comprehensive approach to learning. I perceive that you, Richard and Melissa, are better educated in this way, and we think that our children would benefit from spending time with you."

"Will you take them under your wings, and discuss with them these matters that interest them, and help them to learn what they cannot learn from me and my wife, and what they cannot learn at school? The children say, Melissa, that you have a simple and beautiful way of explaining profound spiritual matters. They talk of nothing at Sunday dinner but what they have learned from you at Sunday school."

"Yes, on two conditions," Richard said.

"Anything, you ask," said the pharmacist.

"First – they can come on Saturdays once they have finished all of their chores at home, but it will be their decision whether or not to come."

"We agree, and secondly?"

"No pay."

"Nothing?" said the pharmacist.

"Can't we share some fresh sausage or other things like that with you from time to time?" asked the wife.

"*German* sausage?" asked Richard, smiling.

"Better than that," stated the pharmacist's wife, "home-made sausage from my brother's farm."

"Agreed," said Richard, "you can send something for us to share at the meal when Mary and Adam visit us."

"The children will be excited, I know; let's tell them!" said the pharmacist's wife.

And so, just over a year ago, they had started their Saturday get-togethers. Richard recalled one time in particular that Melissa had been working with the young brother and sister on the topic of mental creation.

She had explained how that all that exists had been created, and that creation always takes place in the same manner. It was possible, she explained, to learn the principles of creation so that we too can create – so that we might participate in the creative act.

This particular session had been just before Richard and Melissa were to leave for France. Melissa had summarized the process of mental creation: "There are the four alchemical elements, as you well know. What are they? Adam?"

"Yes, that is correct; Air, Fire, Earth, and Water. Now, Mary, in what sequence do they appear, from the most subtle, to the most dense?"

"That is correct; Fire is the most subtle, and in increasing density follow Air, Water and Earth. And what is the fifth element, or fifth essence?"

"Yes, Mary, it is the Quintessence. Now when you form in your mind the ideal that is to become manifest, what element would that be? Adam?"

Adam cleared his throat and spoke. "It would be the Quintessence; this is the most celestial, the most heavenly of them all. In a way, it is the Divine Mind itself, in which everything, including the other elements has its source."

"Very well stated, Adam," said Melissa, "and absolutely correct, insofar as the limits of our words and thoughts can express attributes of the Divine. Richard has an old manuscript that I think expresses this well. I suggest that you copy this in your notebooks, but for now, please listen intently, and you can copy the words while I am preparing dinner."

"For each and every created thing, the Quintessentia is its power, its quality and its virtue. Therefore consider the Quintessentia as comprising a fifth element that is within all matter. As such, it forms an ultimate foundation, from which flow the four

discernible lower elements: fire, water, air and earth.
These four elements may be regarded as being the
abode of the Quintessentia. The Quintessentia is a most
subtle essence, permeating all things, and which,
although it lies hidden within each and every substance,
may nevertheless be made perfectly discernable."

"Now, what is the next step in creation, after the formation of the ideal in the mind? Mary?"

Mary opened her eyes, "It is desire. This is most like the Fire element, I think. This means that it is necessary to have some strong impulse to set things into motion, just as Aries, the sign of Spring is a fiery sign."

"Very good, Mary." Melissa said. "Then, what is the next step?"

"It is the clear mental creation of the condition or thing desired using the full power of the imagination, as you have shown us to do when we paint a mental image one detail after another until the image is complete."

"Then, Mary, what element would this be?" asked Melissa.

"It would be Air, because it is the next element in sequence of density."

Melissa pressed on: "That is good reasoning, but not all good reasoning will lead us to find a truth. Why, do you think it is so?"

Adam suppressed a laugh, blurting out, "Well, mental activity is sort of 'airy', and my sister has a head full of it at times!"

Mary turned red, and then began to laugh with the others, then said quite seriously, "That's not quite fair. I don't know why Air is related to the visualization part of mental creation."

"Mary, it is not so important to memorize the facts, not like learning when the Battle of Hastings took place, or who signed the Magna Carta. What is important is to have useful questions that we can ponder and assimilate in our own way, and at our own pace. You should enjoy working with this sort of question, and the answers that you find will be your own," said Melissa. Then turning to Adam, she asked, "All right, comedian, what is the next step?"

Adam stood and stretched his arms above his head, and when seated answered, "It is the step of 'living in the dream', or emotionalizing about the mental creation. It is an important step, because, in it, one begins to 'feel' the creation, and this gives much energy, much vitality to it. The element would definitely be Water, the element of feelings and emotions." Adam seemed pleased with his answer.

"Very good. And what is the next step? It obviously corresponds in some way to the Earth element, so what is the last step of creation? Adam? Mary?" Melissa asked the question and remained silent, even though no one answered. Mary and Adam looked at each other and them back to Melissa.

Mary spoke first. "I thought we had covered it all. I don't recall a missing step from our previous conversations on mental creation."

Then Adam, "We don't know, Melissa, so what is it?"

"It is an important step, but perhaps it didn't seem like a step at all in our previous discussions. It is really quite easy to miss," Melissa said evenly.

"Remind us again, please, Melissa." Adam said, quietly, eyes fixed on her. "We really do try and pay attention, and review our notebooks and do our exercises. We just thought that you do the other steps, and the creation simply takes place. I thought it was just that simple. The Earth element could represent the final manifestation, so what else is missing?"

Melissa leaned across the table, putting her face near Adam's. "All right, now. Listen carefully. Imagine that you have been helping Richard to cut wood for the entire morning, and as the sun climbed in the sky, it became hotter by the moment. When you come inside, you are so parched that you drink four glasses of my iced tea one after the other, and you sit in the chair to rest but are so tired that you fall into a deep sleep. Mary wants to play a trick on you, and without waking you, she puts your hand into a bowl of warm water. What happens?"

"I pee all over myself?" asks Adam, thinking this a strange turn of conversation.

"Exactly!" exclaims Melissa, now upright in her seat. "And how did you do that?"

"Well, I just let go," said Adam.

"Right. That is the last step. You have to 'let go'. Do you understand now?" asked Melissa, turning to Mary and then to Adam, and then smiling.

By now, all four of them were laughing. "I think I'm going to wet myself now!" cried Mary, doubled over in laughter.

"Just 'let go' Mary," Adam said, imitating the tone and rhythm of Melissa's voice.

While Melissa prepared dinner, Mary and Adam copied from the manuscript on the Quintessence into their notebooks, and Richard helped in the areas where the manuscript was unclear from age, or from unfamiliar spellings. Then, Adam and Mary summarized in their own way the steps of mental creation and how they related to the elements.

After dinner, they asked the brother and sister to keep an eye on their place while they were in France, and began to pack so they might leave on Monday morning.

Richard and Melissa traveled to Mont Saint Michel in Normandy where a number of small groups from the Brotherhood joined together for a conference.

According to the old stories, at the beginning of the 8th Century, St. Aubert, the bishop of Avranches was instructed by the Archangel Michael to build a church on this tiny rocky island. Apparently Michael found the bishop to be too close-minded, for after Aubert ignored the angel's instructions one time too many, Michael burned a hole in the bishop's skull with his finger.

The abbey here remained an important point for contacting telluric currents, forces similar to magnetism that affect the consciousness. The transept crossing was placed exactly at the top of the mount, and it was here that they came to stand quietly for a few moments on the morning after their arrival. The effect could be subtle, or quite suddenly one could feel a radical change in their energy, such as feeling themselves lifted up to the heavens for a moment before being plunged back into their body without warning, so that they struggled not to lose their balance. Afterwards, they would sit silently on one of the benches for a time, and then go back out the entrance to the courtyard, and enjoy the view and invigorating sea air.

The conference sessions were held in large room above a popular restaurant. The owner was an acquaintance of Siegfried, who had procured for him fine antiques for his several restaurants and his home. He took pains to assure the group's privacy, and to prepare wonderful food. Richard enjoyed the *agneau de pré-salé*, a specialty of the area; the lambs that grazed on the salt marsh meadows had an inimitable savor.

During the conference, they were able to meet several members who practiced alchemy, and were amazed at the great ingenuity that they showed in solving technical problems in the laboratory, as well as in solving the riddles and puzzles of the Work. It was as though something in the soil in France provided its people an ability to work with great seriousness in matters of natural philosophy, art, and invention, and yet to enjoy every little pleasure of life with great enthusiasm.

On the morning of their departure, Richard shared his observation with one of their alchemical companions. René replied, "It is not a joke, my friend! There is indeed something special; it is the *silex*, or flint in the ground. Perhaps after a thousand incarnations or so, you will have evolved sufficiently to become French yourself, and to assist you in that, I have a medicine for you. When your palate will become more sensitive, you can perhaps taste the flint in this." He held out two fine bottles of Sancerre sauvignon. "This is a special wine of the Loire, bottled on an estate very near to my home."

A moment later, Pierre Benoît arrived and pressed a packet under Richard's arm. "It is something for you; perhaps you will find it of some benefit. Do you have a copy of *Coelum Philosophorum*?"

"By Paracelsus? No, I don't have a copy, although I have read ..."

"This is not the book of Paracelsus having a similar title, but rather the work of Ulstadius, which will give you many useful ideas concerning the work you have recently started."

After bidding *adieu* to friends new and old, Richard and Melissa started their long journey home.

They had started unpacking their bags, glad to be in their cottage, eager to sleep in their own bed that night. Melissa had checked on her garden, and saw that

Mary and Adam had been there and had freshly swept the front steps after pulling the weeds. The house had also been aired out and the windows were open, and the mail stacked neatly on the table.

It was Mary who appeared at the door first, apparently agitated. "How was your trip? Did everything go well?" It was apparent to both Melissa and Richard that she had something entirely different in mind. Adam was behind her, only the top of his head, a blond mop, visible.

"Come on in and sit down," Melissa said, pointing to the bench.

Richard watched, amused as the two virtually jumped to the bench, sitting as upright as statues. Nervous statues, at that, he thought.

"Adam and I tried the mental creation method. It *works*," said Mary, the tone of her voice relaying alarm.

"Of course it works," said Melissa. "When you set into motion…"

"How do you get it to *stop*?!" Mary interrupted.

"Let's start from the beginning," Melissa said quietly, evenly, as she moved to the bench next to Mary. "What did you set about to create?"

"He had better tell you. Adam?" Mary nudged her brother across the table.

Adam stood up, and began. "I wanted some laboratory equipment. Just a few bottles, and flasks and things. Retorts. Mary and I discussed it – we both wanted it."

"And what did you do next?" asked Melissa.

"Well I created it all in my mind. A laboratory. And then I saw myself using the equipment, and doing things to help other people with it. I was in the middle of the laboratory. Mary was there too, working with me, and we were working with the herbs like Richard showed us – making a plant elixir. It was really exciting."

Richard sat on the bench beside Adam, and asked, "So, what is the problem, Adam?" Melissa could see that Richard was amused, even though Adam was still a bit agitated.

"The stuff shows up on our doorstep. People drop things off at the pharmacy. I had told Father that we wanted some things, thinking that maybe he would have some glassware that he didn't need. Mary also mentioned this to one of the teachers at school. But we don't know where it is all coming from! There are boxes and boxes of stuff. People we haven't seen for years have heard from some neighbor or another that we need things for a school project. Our father doesn't even have as much stuff as this; anyway, he gave us most of what he had left over from university." Adam paused, and then turned to Melissa. "How do we get this to stop?"

Richard and Melissa started to laugh, which didn't help Adam's mood. Mary stood up and touched Richard and Melissa on their shoulders. "This is serious, Richard. Melissa! What if it doesn't stop?" They stopped laughing, realizing that Mary was frightened.

"How big was this laboratory you imagined, Adam?" asked Richard as Mary returned to her seat.

"Like yours," Adam replied, not looking up. "And when I saw it, there was always sunlight in the room, like from a sky light."

Melissa spoke next. "Well, do you have room for a laboratory of that size?"

"We didn't," Mary explained, "but now Father and Mother are thinking of letting us set up the laboratory in the store room at the back of the pharmacy – and there is a sky light. Father says that it reminds him of his school days, and that he might even want to work with us sometimes. Adam and I don't know how to stop this."

"It will stop on its own when it is time," said Melissa firmly. "Just stop thinking about this; in particular stop worrying about it. Just relax. Accept what you have set into motion and quit focusing on it. If you had wanted a laboratory for purely selfish reasons, I don't think it would have developed quite this far. That fact that you both worked on the creation is an important fact, as well as the motivation of helping others with your work."

Richard excused himself from the table, and returned from the laboratory with a box and set it by the front door. "Here are some things for the two of you. There is another box back in the lab as well. We set these aside for you before we left for our trip, to show our appreciation to you for watching the house while we were gone."

It was a box overflowing with laboratory equipment, including two nice retorts, wrapped in butcher paper. Mary shook her head and then leaned on Melissa's shoulder and hugged her. Adam blanched. "Thank you," he whispered.

"Don't mention it", said Richard, smiling.

Chapter 3

*That which the dream shows is the shadow of such wisdom
as exists in man, even if during his waking state he may
know nothing about it... We do not know it because we are
fooling away our time with outward and perishing things,
and are asleep in regard to that which is real within ourself.*

- Philipus Aureolus Paracelsus (1493 - 1541)

These memories had come to Richard as he sat in his chair, and he enjoyed the opportunity to reflect on the experiences that he and Melissa had shared with their eager students. They had come so far in a short time! Of course, they had taken the maximum advantage of their weekly sessions, had studied the loaned books, performed the suggested exercises, and had asked excellent questions. It seemed that they had grown in maturity and stamina to an extent that they rivaled some of his and Melissa's peers in the Order.

In fact, he could have easily thought of a dozen adults, in the so-called advanced grades of study that had failed utterly and completely to grasp certain fundamental principles of occult work. They had become the rule rather than the exception as the weakening of the Order had progressed to a state that foretold its ultimate collapse.

Disharmony. Financial ruin. Despair. How could such qualities be characteristic of the most powerful exponent of the 'Mysteries' known to modern man? He knew all too well that it can be no other way – in some manner, the body will become polluted by outside influences, will be tempted to engage in political concerns, will become increasingly effective in the physical realm and then will cease to be a fit vehicle for the original spiritual ideals. Then, if all goes well, it will die out completely within a few years. Some little vestiges of the Order's activities will have a sort of life of their own, and will continue until the last of the dedicated workers have passed on.

What a pity when the soldiers cannot see that the war is over, that the fight is won, and that it is time to move on.

But, there are some few in every age that are more zealous than insightful. What a noise they make!

What a stench they create around the good name of the Order. It would be more merciful, more dignified if everyone could agree that the active cycle was ended, that it was time to 'give up the ghost' and yet he had not heard of such taking place.

This time the corpse, rotting and wrapped in the ghoulish shroud of the grave, had demanded the unquestioning loyalty of its half-witted supporters, from the highest ranking officers to the newest neophytes. They had raised finances for expansion; they had held drives for membership. The corpse had managed for a time to suck some vitality out of its new adherents, but they found the teachings to be confused, and their superiors to be self-righteous parodies rather than the adepts of Hermeticism that they were supposed to be. They held classes for the general public that caused the Order to be considered one of the least convincing among those groups peddling fraudulent teachings. For this, at least, we can be thankful!

Could anyone in their right mind not see? They should know the tree from its fruits. Where were those members who were capable of being the representatives of the Divine on the earth? New members asked and the public asked, and the smug superiors must have asked themselves the same question. Their response – 'you must become more worthy yourselves, to attract the attention of the Unknown Superiors – the exalted ones that guide the Brotherhood'. This may have worked if there was any evidence that the leaders of the organization had themselves attained to any state of worthiness above that of the general populace.

And what were these superiors of the Order like? They stood out from the common people. They were arrogant, and scorned the values of society. They cited arcane babble about the various occult bodies of man, and hinted that they possessed the Great Arcanum of the Philosopher's Stone. They had cabala babble and karma babble and they exuded bombastic litanies about the Divine and its workings. They preached about the Brotherhood's great minds of the past, and glorified the name of the Order with trite legends, unsupported by facts. When questioned about this, they replied from behind their impenetrable veil that vulgar history had not yet caught up with the 'secret history' they were entrusted with preserving.

In short, they fashioned the corpse into a dancing marionette and tried to amuse a disinterested people.

The few blindly devoted apostles managed to do little to improve on this ridiculous likeness that they had presented to the public, and their books, purporting to teach the true methods of the Brotherhood were as asinine as any such book had ever been in the past. Hopefully, due to the cheap grade of paper on which they had been printed, these anti-manifestos would have turned to dust by the time that this country was ready to herald in another rebirth of the Order.

Of course, the time would come. Once again, the call would go out on the subtle level, and some souls would respond to it, recognizing the perennial proclamation that it was time to summon all brothers and sisters of the Order. At that time, the Work would again convene in the outer world. There remained nothing to do but wait for that time. There were many, like Richard and Melissa, who kept relatively quiet, living unobtrusively in their communities. They had nothing to do with the dying organization, and generally, gave it little thought. They lived in the present, and worked for the future.

From time to time, they were contacted by those who were attracted by their manner, who found comfort in their company. These few were instructed, usually without mention of the source of their knowledge, in some basic principles that would assist them in living more fulfilling lives. Some of these had suspected that there was a hidden source for the teachings, and had ardently sought after it.

Melissa had first revealed something of the nature of the Order to Mary and Adam just this Spring. They had been unaware of the declining reputation of the Order in various nearby countries. Here, the Order was essentially unknown. Richard and Melissa had been comfortable here in a country relatively unaffected by the decaying Brotherhood.

In a short time, the Order would be made visible in this country; it had been nearly 100 years since it had been active here. Prior to 'going dark', the seeds had been planted. These needed to be nurtured, to be protected. There was always work to be done. The image of the worker in the vineyard was a poignant symbol. Long ago, Richard had asked to be shown where to work, and had promised to toil for as long as he lived; his offer had not gone unheeded.

Richard was sitting quite still, his body entirely relaxed. He had allowed his thoughts to run wild for a time. Long ago he had found that to resist the mind takes precious energy. Watching his thoughts as though they were those of a stranger, he had let them run free, allowed them to play themselves out, so as to dissipate any concealed emotional disturbance.

Finding himself at peace with his task in life, he began to clear his mind, and habit took over. His breathing became gentle and even, and he became aware of the immortal part of himself, the underlying and genuine essence which was at one with all that is. Without a struggle, the outer mind relaxed, and there were no more thoughts to think. There was only being. In this being, he was utterly centered, no longer Richard, no longer a man, no longer any particular thing.

His eyes opened slowly. Richard felt his heartbeat, it was strong and vital. He was inspired as well, and felt ready to commence his work for the day. He knew not where it would lead, for long ago he had begun to hold little concern for the details of his work, trusting that all would proceed as required if he focused on the inner qualities of that which he was directed to do.

Oh yes! He felt directed. It was as though there was a wave, a powerful surging of an eternal ocean of consciousness. The wave had motion, and it had direction. It had power beyond his finite comprehension. It would carry him rather than crush him; it would bathe him rather than drown him.

Like the gentle arms of the mother, like the powerful arms of the father, it carried him, filling his lungs with the rarefied air of the eternal. He need not attempt to direct the wave – such was unthinkable! He and the wave were as one; its direction and his had been ordained from the instant before time began. In the grasp of a deep and primeval rhythm, they eluded time; they lived and breathed in caressing waves of divine love and divine devotion. It had always been so.

He knew that he and Melissa were part of the same eternal sea, traveling on waves that were connected by the same primal water of life and consciousness. He was content that they were on different waves, for as such they joined their distinct hues in the lush and immense orchestration sounding the eternal *AUM*.

With this thought, he began to hear traces of the silence behind all terrestrial sound, and in it he heard his own voice merging with that of Melissa, with the rich colors of his various initiators, with those of his parents, with that of the unseen Inner Master. The whole of the sea sang for him, and he felt it bathing all of creation, penetrating to the core of every sentient being, to the marrow of each stone and flower, to the very heart of the Sun and the invisible sun.

All shone with the ineffable streams of light that radiated from each and every point. All reflected the all. Aspiring to look behind the myriad of images, past the appearance of even these celestial images, he felt the resonance of the Word in the very core of his being, and all that he beheld became Fire. There were no points, no edges, no streams, and nothing more to appear. Divine Light and Love vitalized and bathed and nursed him, embracing him and he felt himself let go.

Melissa felt a surge of energy, and knew that her husband had finished his morning devotion. He would soon start to prepare the laboratory for more subtle work. He had spent months preparing the antimony that he was working on, and she had helped him at times. It was tedious work. He had been receiving shipments of ore from various places, and after a number of tests had decided on a location in Romania as the best source.

Then the two of them had begun the tedious process of finely grinding the ore. They had risen each morning and put on the oldest clothes they had. After meditation and a light breakfast, they started to work on the brittle black stones. They covered their faces with wet handkerchiefs and tied rags around their shoes to avoid contact with the toxic dust. The effects of poisoning might be diarrhea, vomiting, nerve damage or worse. They looked like two dirty waifs, like leprous beggars. Working slowly, so that they could continue for several hours, they took turns breaking the ore with the hammer, and dumping the pieces into a bucket for the other who worked it with the heavy iron mortar and pestle. After they had tired of their respective tasks, they traded places. For variety, when they had processed thirty or forty pounds of ore, a day's work, they started to sift the ore with a screen, and separated the coarse material from the finer dust. The larger pieces were returned to the mortar and ground again. It had taken nearly a week to process just over two hundred pounds of ore.

Richard had then set out in an even more tedious process, that of making regulus, or pure antimony. He had managed to come up with an efficient way of working with the ore and was able to make nearly sixty-five pounds of purified regulus in two weeks, with Melissa helping for part of each day. He had worked for ten to fifteen hours every day, except for the Saturdays when Adam and Melissa came. Those were his days for rest, and he often slept until early afternoon on Sunday. Then, after dinner, he would return to his work. Melissa had worried about him, knowing that it did little good to scold him, or to warn him of overtaxing himself.

After the two weeks were completed, he agreed to take a rest, and he didn't go into the lab for several days. They took walks; he helped Melissa with her herbs. Finally Richard announced that it was time to 'marry Luna to the dragon'.

This was again a tedious task. The large supply of silver from her father's estate provided the more than thirty pounds of the precious metal that were required.

Richard soon looked even wearier than before. Finally, though, he emerged from the laboratory, triumphant but obviously weak. This had involved fusing the silver with antimony in the intense fire, the crucible glowing yellow-white, at times seemingly translucent. Toxic white smoke seethed forth with each new spoonful of the niter that he added cautiously to purify the regulus.

Then followed a Herculean task: shattering and then grinding this new mixture, harder than antimony by an order of magnitude, and passing it through screens and re-grinding the coarse portion until all was as fine as face powder. This, heavy grayish powder was the *lunar martial regulus of antimony*, which could now transfer its energy to purified metallic mercury where it would accumulate through tedious repetitions of amalgamation and distillation.

Richard had managed to put a motor on the mortar and pestle to raise and drop the heavy pestle as the mortar turned around slowly below it. The idea had come to him as they rode a train when traveling to France, inspired by the continuous pounding of the wheels on the steel rails. This reduced much of the labor required to powder the alloy, but it still required attention at all times.

At last he announced to himself, that 'the marriage was complete' and that there was 'only one more portal before we try to fly Eagles with it'. He slept for a full day and night.

Richard shook the sleep from his brain, and sat up in the bed. It was late and the house was still. Their room was full of pale light. He searched vainly to see if the moon was shining into the room, and recalled that the moon was now just a crescent and besides, the shades were closed. The light was pale, of a deep violet hue, scintillating and moving in slow currents. He looked down at his hands, and saw that his aura, the light shining from his body, was intensely violet. There were cool flames of light streaming forth from his fingertips. Amused, he held the tips of the forefingers close together, and then pulled them apart, watching the aura stretch like rubber bands between them. He fanned the fingertips of one hand past the others and watched the little elastic bands of light as they jumped along.

Melissa was deep in sleep beside him, beautiful and innocent as a child. She was also bathed in the violet light. It was as though the two of them were streaming forth light and filling the room, to its very corners. He hummed to himself, and watched the light start to ripple, saw it begin to shimmer in response to the sound. In his mind, he sounded the password of the highest degree of the Order to which he had attained, sounding it clearly as though it was being spoken by the richest and most sonorous voice imaginable.

The light became more intense, and now contained flecks of lavender, indigo and white. It began to coalesce some six feet in front of him, in the center of the room.

Slowly, the form of his mentor, the humble teacher of chemistry, Professor Karl Koenig, became discernible in the gently rotating whirl of light. As his form became clearer, Richard had to fight to maintain consciousness. He felt so tired; he should be asleep now. When he attempted to focus clearly on the apparition, it began to disintegrate. He was walking a tightrope: he could not relax too much and could not concentrate too much or he would miss an extraordinary event. Never had his friend appeared to him in this way!

He felt Melissa begin to stir, and he realized that she was fully awake and aware of the presence of her father.

The voice of his mentor, as delicate and clear as it had been in life, impressed itself in his consciousness. "I bid you Peace. Do not tarry in your work... the time is auspicious for flying the eagles until the Full Moon... I will be with you again..."

The words felt like a warm, moist vibration deep inside his brain, as though a moth was attempting to take flight from the very center of his skull. It was at once comforting to hear his beloved friend and unnerving to hear without his ears.

Richard slipped into unconsciousness, into the bliss of silent sleep. He never thought to respond, never thought to question the circumstances of the Professor's brutal death.

Chapter 4

In summer, the song sings itself.
- William Carlos Williams (1883 - 1963)

Not long after he and Melissa had met, they knew that they were going to spend their lives together. Due to their ages, and the uncertainty of Richard's future, they hesitated at first to openly discuss the matter of how they would begin a life together. Melissa's father needed her in their home, and she was an officer in a very vital lodge of the Order, and would soon be expected to serve for a time in its highest administrative and teaching role. Richard had only now entered the 'inner circle' of the Order, and would begin the demanding studies that were required of him.

The idea that they should fall in love, much less decide to marry anyone, had been far from their thoughts. But, they knew that this was to be, and each wanted it with the whole of their heart and mind. Everything seemed to fit together, and while they were careful to 'make haste slowly', they felt as if a guiding hand had revealed the way to become more of themselves, of their real selves, by joining together.

Richard was living with his uncle while in school; the income from his parents' estate would allow him to stay in school until he could begin a medical career. Melissa on the other hand was accustomed to living in a rather leisurely lifestyle; her main work consisted in caring for her father. Richard considered that Melissa might not be willing to live as a pauper while he continued school and served as an intern.

Nonetheless, they announced to Melissa's father their intent to be married. He was genuinely glad for both of them, and explained that he could not imagine any happier outcome for the two of them, but he did take time on the next evening to discuss with them the details of their financial condition, as well as Richard's plans for the future.

The Professor indicated that he had developed a great love for Richard and welcomed him as a son, and that he would be honored if he could pay for the wedding himself and provide them a good start in life.

And so, Richard and Melissa were wed, in the very lodge where they had, at different times, become initiates of the higher grades of the Brotherhood. Richard's uncle Stephen, Siegfried and others had attended the wedding.

The Professor requested that Richard and Melissa might continue to live with him 'for a short time, two weeks or so, as I have arranged to fix up the old house in town as a gift to the two of you'. This was a small one-story house where Melissa had been born; her parents had first lived here when they came to work at the university. Melissa's father had kept it, partly out of sentimentality, partly as a storehouse for chemicals and some of her mother's things that he couldn't bear to discard.

Their new home was at the other end of the block. Melissa was relieved that Richard found the arrangement agreeable – their house was close enough that she could continue to look in on her father each day, and yet she could begin her new life with her husband.

Richard decided that this was a wonderful opportunity for him as well – he would be able to continue his studies in alchemy with the Professor.

While he was deeply moved to relieve those suffering from diseases, to comfort them, he knew that he could accomplish as much or more through the alchemical work as he could with a medical practice. Just as the lowliest of weeds along the roadway, rightly chosen and prepared, could heal as well as the most costly of the pharmacist's offerings and often more safely, so could an alchemist contribute to man's well being just as well as a physician. And so, Richard decided, after consulting with Melissa, to stop his medical education for the time, and devote his time to her, and to his alchemical studies.

This decided, he began a new life as an initiate – a person truly reborn, having now started a new life. He was fully committed to his newly revealed mission, and had now joined his life with that of the remarkable woman with whom he would share all of life's joys and trials.

Chapter 5

I am among those who think that science has great beauty.
A scientist in his laboratory is not only a technician: he is
also a child placed before natural phenomena which impress
him like a fairy tale.

- Marie Curie (1867 - 1934)

Soon after the wedding, Professor Karl Koenig resumed the tedious process of instructing his son-in-law in laboratory alchemy. This task was made easier by the young man's passion; he would be required to work hard for his knowledge. He observed that Richard was painstaking in the laboratory, making careful observations and that often he could 'intuit' the best options to proceed in his work. He quickly adapted the symbolism of qabala and of classical mythology as means to solve alchemical puzzles. Perhaps most telling, Richard looked to Nature as the Great Teacher, the Great Revelator.

The youth's most apparent flaw was that he relied too much on his memory; he did not take notes extensively. Perhaps he was over confident in his power of observation and his ability to remember what he had read. The work in the laboratory can be so enthralling that one loses track of time, and the body will become increasingly out of balance, affecting the senses, the mind and judgment.

As a young novice, while studying with a series of instructors, Karl had filled volumes with notes; often these included quite detailed sketches of apparatus and narratives of what was seen, as well as what he felt inwardly. This habit he had maintained throughout his life. In his own laboratory, everything was painstakingly labeled – even small vials and envelopes containing alchemical products or ingredients were numbered and could be cross-referenced to the proper notebook to explain what the substance was, or through what process it had been prepared.

This young man would have to learn the need for the habit, as it was not his inclination apparently! The older man did not need to wait long for an opportunity to make this point effectively.

One night he found Richard furiously at work, and, of all things, writing notes! "So, young man, you do know how to write after all! What are you working on?"

"Nothing important, Professor. Just some tests."

"And you take up writing notes for some 'unimportant' tests?"

"If you must know, I am trying to sort out what I did to get this!" Richard indicated a shallow dish, its bottom covered with small emerald-green crystals. "I had calcined either galena, or lead carbonate ore, and treated it with acetum, and I am unsure which. Perhaps I had moved things around as I was working on several different substances during the evening. I didn't expect to see this. There was nothing green anywhere before this acetic extract evaporated; in fact the tincture was more orange-red when I filtered it. Of that, I am quite certain! Still, Professor – it is quite beautiful, no?"

"Perhaps it is all right to work on a number of things, but everything should be labeled and referenced in the laboratory notes."

"Professor, do you know what this is from? Can you just tell me?"

"To the former question, 'yes', and to the latter, 'no'. When you figure it out you will know one of them".

"One of what?"

"One of the so-called 'Green Lions' that your favorite author Weidenfeld described and which can be used to produce a powerful solvent. You should consider yourself fortunate to have found something so useful. It is almost certain that you will rediscover it someday. Good night, Richard"

"Good night, Professor. Is it really a green lion? Professor? …. Professor!"

Within two years of first coming to live here, Richard had surpassed the other novices. His hands were a testament to his progress: from the continual washing of glassware, tables, benches, and floors, his hands were chronically dry, although he had some relief from an extract he made from egg yolks, and essential oils of lavender blended in lanolin. Oil of lavender was kept within reach to dab on the inevitable burns and small cuts.

Richard had once theorized a way to prepare a plant stone of rosemary. It was a long work, which involved imbibing the heated plant salts of the herb with the liquid tincture extracted from the herb with highly rectified spirit of wine. The mixture was held in a delicate ceramic crucible over a burner flame. The experiment was left running whenever he was in the laboratory, and when he was at a convenient breaking point in whatever other work he conducted, he would follow a routine: lift the crucible cover with tongs held in his left hand, and from a dropper in his right, he added tincture until the greenish-black powder in the crucible was a moist paste. Then he would replace the crucible cover.

The fragrance was piercing when the tincture was first added, from the essential oil of rosemary that he used to fortify the tincture; in the parlance of an alchemist, he had added more volatile sulphur. He had also added the volatile salts captured during the initial calcination of the plant remains once the tincture had been extracted. These were two ways he had proposed to speed the formation of the stone.

One night, exhausted and ready for sleep, Richard had lifted the crucible lid, prepared to dispense the forest-green tincture, and realized that he was looking straight into the bottom of the crucible, through a transparent liquid, glowing yellow-orange from the heat of the flame. His stone had found the balance of the three principles! It was no longer a greenish-black volcanic lump; it was clear and molten! Now he would pour it into the small mold that he had begun to heat, and allow it to cool slowly. He was about to cast a plant stone!

As Richard set the dropper back into the bottle of tincture, he had unconsciously relaxed his grasp on the tongs, and the crucible cover struck the slate bench top and bounced like a coin, amazingly unbroken. Instinctively, he grabbed it mid-bounce with his right hand; the result was a blackened brand spanning two of his fingers in a circle, and more painful yet, a spot in the center of his palm where the outer layer of skin pulled away when he dropped the glowing lid. He quickly poured lavender oil over his palm and fingers, which immediately drew out most of the heat. He would be applying it for days! Despite his painful wound, he had calmed himself to pour the stone of rosemary into the mold and set in an oven where it could cool slowly overnight.

He had taken Melissa and the Professor to see the stone the next morning. During the night, he had awaken to turn off the oven so that the stone would cool to the touch. Now freed from the mold, the stone was the size of a pigeon's egg, white with two pale blue streaks. The Professor touched the stone to his tongue, and pronounced that it should be quite medicinal when applied to matters related to the Sun, for example blood pressure, the heart, the eyes. It should be more useful to the person who made it for use as an initiatic medicine – that is, a medicine that would provide the body with the specific frequencies of energy to bring their consciousness to the next level of evolution. This was a little-known function of the medicines of the alchemists: to transmute the body and mind of the alchemist themselves. These same medicines had little 'initiatic' effect on the average person, in which case they were chosen to correct the causes for illness, or to strengthen the nerves or an organ.

To test of the power of the stone, the Professor had directed Richard to secure the stone with a waxed thread, and to immerse it in a beaker of distilled water with some fresh rosemary floating on the surface. Moments after the stone was submersed, held an inch below the floating herb, tiny rivulets of green began to stream down from the herb, from many points, and they began to coalesce and form a cloudy condition at the same level as the suspended stone. The Professor clapped Richard on the shoulder, "Take the stone out now, and carefully blot it without putting much pressure on it. Let it dry carefully, and then keep it in a sealed jar. I suspect it is not fully balanced; the salt will drink in moisture, even from the air. Still, it is quite well done. You may be able to cure it somewhat by adding pure oil of rosemary to it with very, very gentle heating. It should not need to be melted and recast again. I suggest that you and Melissa drink the water from our experiment some little time before you meditate tonight. Maybe you will get some idea of the usefulness of such a stone for initiatic purposes. You might have, for example, unique dreams that can reveal interior teachings and deepen your understanding of the inner realms. As you well know, rosemary is a Solar herb. You might consider preparing some additional stones, from plants ruled by the Moon, Mercury, and Saturn to use in this way. The Mars and Jupiter stones are likely not so useful for you. And Venus, also less useful.

At home, Melissa explained that the precious essence of the everlast flower, *Helichrysum italicum*, would erase all scarring from Richard's wound. "After it is well healed and no infection is present, use this sparingly, dilute it in some lavender oil if you like".

Richard had been pleased to move his experimental work to the Professor's private laboratory. The invitation had come after the successful plant stone work.

When Siegfried's travels permitted it, he would join them. About once a month Siegfried would come for lunch on a Friday and visit through the weekend. A portion of the time was spent in laboratory work, although Melissa would insist on the gentlemen stopping their labors and dressing properly for a leisurely Saturday evening meal. Richard was pleased to hear any news from his uncle, and all were eager to hear news about the affairs of the Order in those countries where the work was still vital, as well as in the places where the work had begun to decay.

The Professor was insistent that the alchemical practices were an essential aspect of the work of the Order, that they were a treasure of inestimable value for

Humanity. As his close friend and his family savored their desert, he elaborated, "The degree of responsibility required to tread the alchemical path is not suitable for persons who have not fully subdued their animal natures. This is why only theoretical principles of alchemy are introduced to students, and only then after some period of trial and testing. There are dangers in the technical work of alchemy, surely, but these are as nothing compared to the dangers of attraction to temporal power and wealth. To offer revelations regarding the path of transmutation to those not prepared has been said to be like unto 'casting pearls before swine'. It is more grievous than this, I fear, as it is not likely the pearls would harm the swine.

"Unfortunate would be the adept whose abilities for healing are suspected outside our circle. What would you give, Richard, to save the life of Melissa from a horrible disease and certain death? I am sure you would do anything and everything for someone you love more than you love yourself. At what point would you stop? Would you exact the healing remedy from an adept by torture if they would not offer you the medicine? Would you threaten their life? It is a dilemma that no one should be faced with.

"I apologize to make such a distasteful example during our happy gathering, I am sorry; I see that I have upset you, Richard. My point is that the utmost in discretion is necessary in such matters, as we should avoid needlessly creating those tempting circumstances that bring peril to the soul of man.

"One of my brothers in our Order told me a story. He was raised in a church that held services on Sunday mornings and on Thursday nights. The church had a historical connection with our Order, he discovered many years later as an adult. The church was a small one, and he often wondered why the gathering on Thursday nights was smaller, and was attended by only a few families. These were in fact families who preserved our work privately during the 'silent time' of the Order in their country.

"When members of this sect became ill, they would naturally go to the village doctor, who was a deacon in the church. He was a homeopath and would carefully question them on many facts seemingly unrelated to their ailment, as is normal for these practitioners to do when selecting a remedy. After some time, he would be satisfied, and perhaps reference a text or two before going to the shelf and selecting a remedy, and then put five or six white pellets under their tongue, and give them a small envelope of the remedy to take at home for several days. His skill was unmatched in selecting remedies, and the cures were always effective. After the brother who had told me this story had become an initiate himself, he was reintroduced to the village physician, who was also an initiate of high standing.

"The doctor now revealed to him that the remedy given was always the same one: it was a miniscule amount of the White Stone of the Philosophers diluted in lactose. The alchemist had managed to treat his patients quietly and with wonderful care, without drawing attention to the real nature of his Art."

Chapter 6

Gold is worse poison to a man's soul, doing more murders in this loathsome world, than any mortal drug.

- William Shakespeare (1564 - 1616)

Or ever the silver cord be loosed, or the golden bowl be broken, or the pitcher be broken at the fountain, or the wheel broken at the cistern.

- Bible, Ecclesiastes xii. 6.

During the next weekend that Siegfried visited, the discussion after dessert concerned the method of Nicholas and Perenelle Flamel for making the Philosophical Stone. Centuries later, Philalethes, and then Isaac Newton had worked in a nearly identical manner, and yet there were particular issues that had been elusive, such as the proper seeding of the mercury once it was animated, and the regimen of the fire to incubate the invisible fire – that mysterious energy – that would lead to the confection of the Red Stone. The three men had solved a number of technical problems during their time working together; this had tried the extent of their combined scholarly and chemical knowledge.

The Professor revealed that he had recently determined one certain solution to these remaining problems, based on a manuscript he had formerly not considered important; he had made the connection while preparing the index that he had shown to Richard when they first met. In fact, this had been his motivation for creating the index. Now he wanted to demonstrate to them a Philosophical Stone – by performing a metallic transmutation.

They could not believe what they had just heard! Neither Siegfried nor Richard had imagined that they would ever see such a demonstration in their lifetime!

The Professor took out his pocket watch, glanced at it, and set it on his napkin. They scarcely noticed as he rose from his chair, and walked briskly toward the back of the house. As they sipped from small glasses of chilled Sauterne, they heard the back door open. After more excited discussion between the men, Richard called for Melissa to come, to hear what her father had told them.

Melissa's scream pierced the night. Siegfried and Richard ran toward her voice thinking she had been injured in the kitchen. Richard was the first to reach her; she fainted in his arms. Siegfried brushed them aside and sprinted out the back door.

Melissa was now moving, trembling, and Richard moved with her to the bench in the kitchen. Her face turned away from his, Melissa rocked back and forth, humming to herself.

Siegfried appeared again, his face ashen. He went to the dining room and returned with snifters of Armagnac, offering one to Richard. Siegfried's face was white.

Not a word was spoken. They knew. He was dead! Our Professor! Our Brother! Our Father! Had there been anything to be done, we would have been doing it. Siegfried would not have left his side! There was a smudge of soot on the right side of his face. A smell, horrible, unspeakable, clung to Siegfried's clothes. There had been a fire! It too must be under control. Richard could not move. They heard firemen arrive and neighbors speaking excitedly from all sides of the house. Draining his glass, Siegfried went out to meet them.

Melissa was still, her head in Richard's lap. He did not dare move for fear of disturbing her, for he could not imagine what state she would be in just a little time from now. Nothing was quite real. It was as though the events were happening to someone else. Richard realized suddenly that he was too agitated to sit, but now the back door opened and Melissa sat upright at the sound of Siegfried's urgent steps.

"Oh, Melissa! Dear Richard! My God! Karl is dead. The police and firemen have arrived." He sat beside Melissa, taking her hand. "When I opened the door, I could see that the shed was on fire, and saw the windows breaking. I could not get very close, as the heat was intense. Your father was burned."

"Was he alive when you..." Richard started.

"No. He was... No, he couldn't have been alive. There was something, perhaps acid fuming from the shed. It seems to have burned out for the most part now. Because of the things stored there, the firemen are concerned that there may be more to come... I don't know what all he has stored there. It is dangerous for them. I...."

"I heard yelling... someone was with Father!" Melissa shouted. "An argument.... Oh, my dear father... Why now? I couldn't take care of him. Siegfried, take care of Father." Melissa collapsed and I carried her to her old bedroom, staying beside her while Siegfried led the investigators to the dining room. The delicate glasses of chilled Sauterne once so cheerful in the candlelight were now dreadful to behold.

The investigators had been quick to determine a preliminary cause of death. There was a single stab wound, quite deep, to the abdomen. Defensive wounds and other evidence pointed to the presence of an attacker. Apparently a lantern had been used to deflect a knife thrust as well. The Professor had not moved after the fire started; they concluded that he was already dead; the fire had likely been set on purpose by the attacker after he had delivered the mortal wound.

There were some flammable liquids and various canisters and bags of chemicals lining the walls of the tightly packed shed. There had not been an explosion as such, but there was sufficient heat to break the windows out of the stone building, and a portion of the roof had collapsed.

The authorities thought that robbery could be a potential motive, as they had found an empty strong box that had fit into a hollow under a now-shattered paving stone in the floor. They had asked Siegfried if it was likely to have contained cash, jewelry, or important documents. Later they would question Richard, and after delaying it as much as possible, they met with Melissa. Siegfried had confirmed that the strong box could have held any of those valuables, but withheld his suspicions that it could have been something of even greater value. After all, the Professor had gone to retrieve the Stone!

After assembling the evidence of the various investigators, the police concluded that the professor had surprised a robber in the shed, and struggled with him, losing his life. There were no suspects other than a roster of known burglars operating around the university neighborhood, but the police made it clear that Melissa, Richard and Siegfried were not suspected of foul play.

The Professor's body had been damaged badly; a mixture of flammable and corrosive liquids had leaked onto the floor, and fueled an intense fire. The family was not asked to view his body, but rather asked about his clothing, and so on. After dental records confirmed his identity, the Professor's remains were cremated.

The funeral had taken place, and nearly three hundred had presented themselves at the church to pay their respects, and to share dinner afterwards. It was explained that the interment would be private, for family only.

At nine that evening, seventy-two men and women, members of the Order, gathered at the university chapel for a memorial service. The Grand Master, Siegfried, spoke of the earthly career of "a great soul who has now quit his mundane profession in order that he might more freely dedicate himself to his true vocation." Formalities of the Order customary to the passing of a Brother or Sister were observed. Such rites made no distinction of any titles or grades.

At Melissa's request, Richard read a poem that she had found in her father's study:

"Do not stand at my grave and weep

I am not there; I do not sleep.

I am a thousand winds that blow,

I am the diamond glints on snow,

I am the sun on ripened grain,

I am the gentle autumn rain.

When you awaken in the morning's hush

I am the swift uplifting rush

Of quiet birds in circled flight.

I am the soft stars that shine at night.

Do not stand at my grave and cry,

I am not there; I did not die."

Despite the late hour, almost a dozen of the family's closest friends met at the Professor's home, and talked into the morning hours. Melissa spoke softly, before she slept, "Richard, as much as I miss my father... it is so deep, this wound, and I have been wounded to depths that I did not know to exist. That much, my love, that much and more, is how much I love you."

The next day, the police returned. While they had been matter of fact when they had previously made their final presentation of the circumstances of his death, it was obvious that they were still shaken by the event. The Professor had been no one in particular to the police; they knew him to be a respectable citizen and teacher. Still, there was a murderer on the loose, and so, with little enjoyment, they questioned Siegfried, Melissa and Richard.

There was no question of foul play by any of this group, the police explained once again, unless they were all three in on it, as there was no way that one of them could have done it without the others knowing it – and, there was no way that Melissa would cover up a murder of her own father. There was no possible benefit to her to participate in such a heinous plot, even though there was a sizeable estate.

Melissa was obviously in such pain that she was near collapse. The search of the Professor's circle of associates, and the police had been thorough, had turned up one individual, conspicuous only by his sudden disappearance.

The man was, although the police did not know of such matters, a member of the Brotherhood. The police confirmed that the man had frequented the Professor's home, and that he was quite wealthy. The man's family had reported him missing the day after the

Professor's murder. They had questioned the family and discovered that the suspect had been diagnosed some months before with a serious illness, and he had become increasingly despondent. It was his family's fear that he had perhaps taken his own life.

The family could not imagine that he was capable of violence; further, he would have no motivation to commit robbery. They had felt helpless as they watched his personality radically change, transformed by the pain and by the horror of the sentence of prolonged suffering pronounced on him by the physicians.

Melissa recognized his name – "Henri Hoffmann! Yes, my father knew him. He was here! Just a few days ago, I came home to find him leaving abruptly. Richard was sleeping at our home while I was bringing in groceries for Father. The man nearly ran me over at the front door! He was angry and pushed past me and hurried down the stairs to the sidewalk without a word, without looking back. Father was upset when I came in, but he didn't want to talk about it then. He was not used to angry people – he has... I mean he had just a small group of friends. Why would anyone ... How could..." She raised her hands, balling them into fists, then slumped on the couch, sobbing.

Siegfried and Richard helped the police to fill in the pieces, although they did not mention the Brotherhood, and were not asked about it.

They explained to the police that they had been discussing a problem concerning Hoffmann the afternoon prior to the Professor's death. Their friend had seemed troubled, uneasy. He had said, "I am in a bit of a quandary with this fellow. He is gravely ill, and he wants to take some of these preparations that we have been discussing." They did not mention that the preparations were alchemical preparations. They did not dare.

They were still in shock. His death had been so unexpected. He was so vital! The Professor had just reached a major stage in his alchemical work; that very night he had intended to demonstrate a transmutation to them.

He had gotten up to go to the shed to get the preparation, and to get a manuscript that he had prepared and had hidden there. Why had they let him go alone? One of them should have insisted on going with him. But, they had not. They had no reason to fear for his safety. They had been so excited about the revelation, they had continued to talk, had scarcely noticed him leaving the room.

"And he told us that Hoffman had been outraged when his demands were refused. 'It is too dangerous. I need to test it further,' that's what he told the man. It was apparently an experimental medicine from the university. The man, Hoffman, had again demanded that the Professor test it on him, and he flatly refused, telling him that he would not participate in poisoning a friend," Richard spoke rapidly.

Siegfried, normally eloquent, spoke as slowly as if he had to invent each word needed to express his thoughts, as though he were reading them through a dark curtain, "Herr Hoffmann", he paused, and stared at his fingernails, "offered him a small fortune, he doubled and redoubled the amount when his advances were refused. Finally, he became threatening, and Karl had to demand that he leave at once. He was told not to return until he could act like a gentleman."

The word had been *brother*, Richard recalled.

"Apparently," Siegfried was now looking straight at the detective, "he did return the other evening; or he sent a ruffian to do his work". More rapidly his words came, now that his emotions were not so easily contained, "If I had been present, I would have terminated his painful existence for him – he had no right... I am sorry! I do not mean that, Dear God, I do not! It is not thinkable that anyone who is a ... who is a civilized man could take the life of another to lengthen his own miserable existence. God forgive us all. I cannot continue. Please gentlemen, I beg your leave."

Siegfried walked painfully from the room, sobbing under his breath.

The police inspector stood up, facing Richard. "I think he is right, young man. Please, take care of your wife, and see to your friend. I think we will not bother you again. It is clear that we have both motive and opportunity elsewhere. Now we must find the suspect and ask him some questions". He extended his hand to Richard.

Richard shook it, and walked the policeman to the front door. "Do you think he is alive?"

The detective stopped. "Perhaps he has already poisoned himself with an experimental medicine. Not that I would shed a tear for him if he has."

Richard nodded. But he knew that he would yet shed many a tear for poor Brother Hoffman; he knew that Siegfried was in absolute anguish over the whole matter as well. Murder was always the most heinous of crimes, a further outrage when brother spills the blood of brother.

This was most unthinkable – a man who has pledged himself to serve Humankind, and taken binding oaths to honor life, and to treat all as brothers and sisters, to render any needed assistance... when the murderer is in the Brotherhood, it is a villainy, a stain on the garment of the Order itself.

Such could not be avenged, for murder does not cleanse, rather it defiles. If, indeed, this man was a murderer, he had severed himself from the Order, just as he had severed the life of his brother. The horror was that they must heal him, must bring him to face himself, and must lovingly assist him in re-embracing Divinity! How cruel was their obligation – they must seek him out as a brother in distress and must bathe his wounds, must clothe him in kindness and love, and must anoint his fevered brow with the ointment of Mercy.

"Sometimes I catch myself wishing for a moment that we were a less merciful lot, Siegfried. I've heard of other kinds of oaths – some men are more Biblical in their justice".

"I know, Richard. I've thought about it all. I feel as though I could flay the murderer with little remorse at times, and yet I know that he is still my brother, I am certain that there is more here than appears to the outer eyes. I have sent a message from my mind to Hoffman's, and I know that we have made contact. He is able to block certain details, which is to be expected. I do not feel that he is in any sort of intense remorse – I am sure of that. He is either innocent, or he is beyond any help of the normal sort. This is all the more reason to forgive him. I also know that he is not in this country, and that he has been to a lodge in another land. I think it is France or Belgium.

"Now that the funeral is over, I will leave, and will make some effort to find him, and then to find the truth of this matter. You must stay here with Melissa. I will return as soon as I have been able to put this matter to rest. I have called a meeting of the Council of the Brotherhood. We must elect a successor for Brother Karl; we must select someone to take his place, though we truly cannot".

Siegfried had left them, and except for the rare visitor, Melissa and Richard had the house to themselves. It was a rambling old house, in spite of the rather compact appearance that it presented to the casual observer. It looked quite narrow across the front, which was made of dark reddish stones. The stairs that led up from the street level to the porch were very broad, which added to the illusion of the house being narrow. All one needed to do to get a real idea of the massiveness of the house was to walk past the meandering vines and over-grown rose bushes that closed around the small gate at the right side of the walk, and to follow the stone path. In a dozen meters, they would come to a large area that served as a loading area for the laboratory. There was a narrow roadway leading into the area from an alley that permitted even heavy crates to be brought in and out.

Adjacent to this loading area there was also a door leading into the cellar, though it was long out of use for storing chemicals – the old shed in the back had become the storage area for the more dangerous materials. To reach that shed, one continued along a wide brick pathway that stayed parallel with the high wooden fence marking the southern boundary of the property.

Abruptly, in another forty meters, the path took a sharp turn to the left, and into the front of the old shed, now a shambles, black soot above the windows, a few shards of partially fused glass, hanging desperately to contorted frames. Blackened stumps of ceiling beams stuck out of the tangle.

The burned out building looked frightful, like a child that had been in a horrible accident, shattered glasses twisted on their wounded face.

Despite its wooded surroundings, cheerful birdbaths, bloom-covered lattices and bushes and flower beds like exploding kaleidoscopes of fragrance and color, whimsically painted elves and sprites of stone, yes despite these things, the shed was a rotted tooth, black, and open to a live nerve. The live nerve was Melissa.

She no longer sat on the screened porch at the back of the house to admire her gardens; she no longer worked on her treasured herbs and the rare flowers. The garden, with its rich smells, textures and sounds had been her elixir – it had been at once her textbook, her medicine, her confessor, her companion, and her personal sanctum wherein she retired for meditation and prayer. Now that she needed it more than ever, she could not bring herself to set foot there.

Richard had understood this at once, and he took his bride to Austria, 'to see the countryside', he had told her. Within a week of the announcement that he was taking her on a trip, she had installed her successor, a very capable young man, in her place as an officer of the lodge, and had given the keys to the back entrance to the laboratory to the group that studied there. Word had come from Siegfried that the group would have to study on its own until such time as a suitable instructor could be located. Melissa had appointed one of the group members, after discussing her choice with Siegfried and Richard, as an interim leader for the group.

They had closed the house securely. She sat longingly in her father's room for a time, and then closed and bolted the door from the inside, to keep it secure from anyone who might try to enter from the laboratory. The most valuable texts from the library had also been locked in her father's now-cluttered room, but Richard had taken a few with him, those of Weidenfeld, Flamel and Hollandus. 'It is best to journey in the company of adepts. Well even if Weidenfeld was not an adept, he was clear'. He also took a set of manuscripts on the qabala.

They had stayed at the home of Richard's uncle for three nights. Melissa had slept much of the time, and Richard had been able to explain to his uncle Stephen all that had taken place since he had left home. Siegfried had not come through here yet, it seemed. They made numerous excursions across the country, returning to his uncle's home for a day or two at a time to see if there was news from Siegfried, and to sleep in familiar surroundings.

Chapter 7

The hour of departure has arrived, and we go our ways - I to die, and you to live. Which is better God only knows.

- Plato

They found a lovely cottage perfectly suited to their needs. They had been trekking across an expansive meadow when the cottage had appeared, hidden from three sides by a stand of trees at the top of a hill. It had not been occupied for some time.

At Melissa's urging, Richard inquired after the owner of the property in the nearby village, and found her at work as a hostess in the village inn. She sat at their table and explained that she was quite willing to sell the property.

The woman had inherited it from her father, whom she had taken care of when he became ill. Now she needed to live in town, and lived in a small room above the inn with her young son. For longer than she cared to remember, two men, who intensely disliked each other, had tried to coax her, threaten her nearly, into selling the farm. She had not sold it because of her hatred for both men. One of them, the father of her son, had abandoned her long ago; the other had spent years trying to cheat her sick father out of his property.

She had prayed for a third buyer, someone who had nothing to do with these men. "I am already far behind in my rent here", she confided, "and I need to pay my bills". Richard intuited that the innkeeper was not likely to throw her out, it was apparent in the way that she spoke openly in front of the man, and in the way that he looked at her; they were lovers.

The young woman rose to return to her work pausing to say that her father had told her what was a fair price to expect for the property. "One of the men has already offered me more than that, the other a bit less. I think the one is thinking that I will be part of the bargain. Still, I want only what is fair, and I will let you have it for what my father would have asked. In fact, if you will have it, I will be glad to let the world know that I have let you have it for less this scoundrel has offered! They are cowards – the both of them! ”

In this way, Richard and Melissa became the newest residents of a sleepy village in Austria, just outside the reach of the growing cities. The villagers warmly accepted them, for they had established their willingness to work along side of their new neighbors.

Melissa soon became the preferred midwife in the village, and often received requests for her services and for her 'magical potions' – herbs and essential oils – from the surrounding villages. She was an avid church member, and anyone who was careless enough to question whether the new woman might be a witch was soon set straight by one of her many friends.

Richard seldom went to the church, but this, too, was accepted. He was of boundless good humor, and worked hard. He often met with the village preacher to discuss 'philosophy and all sorts of things,' according to the minister. "He is a good man and lives what he believes. I would certainly call him a Christian man". That was enough for anyone, apparently.

The truth of the matter was that both Richard and Melissa felt little need for the outer rites of religion.

Melissa needed the chance to meet people, to talk, and to get news on how her many 'patients' were doing. Richard preferred to sit quietly or read, and he cultivated fewer contacts, as his work was done in private. The carpenter who had helped him to add the workshop, the postman, and the pharmacist would drop by from time to time, or receive a visit. He sometimes helped the carpenter to carry shingles, or to plane boards while they talked. He made suggestions for new herbal blends to the pharmacist, and gave each of them bottles of herb-infused May wine that he prepared late in the Spring.

The postman would often sit and eat lunch with Richard when Melissa was away in the village or gathering herbs in the fields. The two would share fresh bread and cheese, and perhaps a glass of the herbal wine. 'A delightful tonic for the spirits' as the postman called it.

Richard would share stories and legends from classical mythology that the young postman would tell his wife and children at night. "They like those old stories, Richard. The wife likes them the best of all. She used to get tired of me having nothing to say after a long day of delivering the mail, but now she asks me if

I've been 'round to see you. The kids too, of course. Lots of times, I've made up my own stories while I'm walking from house to house, and just changed around and mixed up some of the characters and things from the other stories. They aren't as good as yours, but they are getting better. My wife can tell when it's your stories that I'm telling, but she likes it when I make up stories for her. She never gets out much, having five young'uns and all. She says that I seem happier. Can a fairy tale make a working man happier? I think so."

And so they continued telling stories to each other. Richard heard from Melissa that the postman was becoming quite popular down at the inn in the village. He was hearing some of the old stories from the old men there, as well, and soon brought those to Richard to swap as well. Mostly these were old ghost stories, and tales of the old families that had settled here, or of the foolishness of the 'citified folks' and tourists who came to the quaint village.

Still, Richard had fully half of each day to himself. He worked incessantly in the laboratory, often well into the night. During the hot part of the day, he sat with Melissa who generally worked with her harvest in the mornings, 'while the dew is still on the meadows, and not yet warmed by the sun'. They worked together, laughing and talking, sometimes making love. Then, as she prepared for the quiet of the evening, after dinner, he resumed his work in the laboratory.

She had seemingly forgotten about the murder of her father, and while Richard knew that she ached to hear his voice, things were going so well for the two of them. Only once or twice had they discussed their life together in the home of her father. Her eyes had become moist when Richard had first mentioned 'the Professor', his mentor, to Adam and Mary.

These two young people had become their friends as much as they were students. Melissa had, through them, come to feel a part of the flow of life, had sensed that the death of her father was in some way a part of Nature's way, just as the disappearance of the delicate blooms in the fields signaled not the end, but rather that the seeds were now safely nestled in the bosom of their eternal mother, awaiting new expressions of life, a life without end.

They had not felt the need to have children of their own, for they sensed in some way that Adam and Mary were their children, that they needed not to become parents in any other way, at least not now. The very idea of dragging a swelling body across the fields each day did not appeal to Melissa. She had cared for many a mother and many an infant. She saw how tired, how spent most young mothers were, even though they were at the height of their physical energy.

Besides, she was, in a manner of speaking, a bride of the Order, and she had given all of her young womanhood over to the tasks of tending the vestal flame, and as she became older, she had worked unceasingly on behalf of the students of the Brotherhood. Now she attempted to realize in the outer world the inspirations that increasingly flowed to her from the quiet urgings of her inner self. She had been fortunate, she thought, to find a fine husband who shared her values and sense of priorities.

From time to time word came from Siegfried, whose travels took him over the whole of Europe in search of fine antiques for his thriving business. An energetic entrepreneur, he had multiplied an already considerable fortune that had long been passed through hereditary lines, as he was not content to be one of the 'idle rich', for whom he had little regard. He had used his wealth to support the various activities of the

Brotherhood. As always, his travels were partly related to his antique business, and partly to the work of the Order.

Siegfried had kept the couple informed by letter as he continued to search for information about the suspected murderer of his dearest friend. His letters explained that some of the jurisdictions of the Order he contacted were dormant, due to political and economic currents in the various regions, and while he was able to make contact with the heads of the Brotherhood, their operations were scattered and it was impossible to find any comprehensive records regarding what traveling members had contacted those small groups that continued to meet.

Some of the groups met in the utmost secret in private homes. They went undetected because their participants might consist of the members of only one or two families. As such they could easily gather without notice. In some cases, the groups were absorbed into lodges of Freemasonry, and in some instances, one might find that a 'discussion group' meeting in a bookstore after hours was the local branch of the Order. It would be possible for a traveling member to make himself recognized by certain signs and passwords, and to be afforded a fraternal welcome.

It would also be very easy for someone to assume an identity, and to make themselves virtually impossible to trace as they moved from place to place. Of course, there was no assurance that our murderer, if indeed he was such, was still in Europe, or even that he would seek out other members of the Order. The police might eventually apprehend the fugitive, but Siegfried needed to alert the scattered members of the Brotherhood that a person concealing his identity might attempt to make contact. Siegfried wrote that one of his first tasks had been warning those who were knowledgeable about alchemical medicines that a sick brother traveling abroad might approach them.

Siegfried poured out his concerns in his correspondence. He had been unable to make further mental contacts with Hoffman. He felt helpless, realizing that it was quite likely that the man had either died from an untreated disease, or that he had been poisoned by the Philosopher's Stone stolen from the Professor. He scarcely dared to consider the alternative. The desperate man may have taken a dose of this transmuting stone, and have been altered by it as the legends would suggest; in such a case, the man would have been physically, mentally and psychically transformed.

If he had taken too large a dose, and being greedy, it was possible, he would have died an agonizing death. If the dose had been right, however, then he would have gone through the classic changes; his hair would have fallen out, and his eyes would become extremely sensitive to light. Likewise, the fingernails and teeth would have fallen out. The thought made him shudder, and he wondered if the transformation was painful. In a few weeks, he imagined, the man would have been more like a new-born infant in appearance, his skin pink, his gums sprouting forth its crop of new teeth, his crown bursting with downy hair. The man may not even look like the one he described to the police: a wretched, ailing man, thin and bent.

What concerned Siegfried more was the idea that a murderer, one who was capable of killing his mentor, might have become one of the few 'ageless ones'. He would surely have undergone a complete rebirth. How would he deal with the remorse, if he indeed had any, if he had to carry it throughout eternity?

It was not true that the immortals lived forever in one physical form; at least this is what he had been told. Rather, they continued in the highest degree of health possible given their heredity and their circumstance, all disease was cast out, and the body sealed against it. Still, they could not make the body an impenetrable castle, for it was material and had certain inherent flaws. What did continue, and forever, was the consciousness of all that they had been, and whenever the adept again incarnated, with them came full recollection of past lives, and full development of their character and psychic power. This is truly what made such individuals powerful and immortal.

The Order had long taught the basic methods of alchemical work, had passed down from the earliest adepts their methods of self-perfection and inner development. Since the beginning, the trials imposed on those who petitioned for access to the mysteries had been of such a nature as to effectively block the progress of those whose motives were less than honorable. How had such a man slipped through?

And it had been in Siegfried's own jurisdiction, in his own lodge that the man had been accepted into the Brotherhood! It was unthinkable, but it had taken place. Now, Siegfried must search for the errant adept, and seek a way to turn him back onto the path that leads to selfless service. This man must be led to forgive himself; there was forgiveness for all who would consciously understand the error of their behavior, who would seek to uproot the weeds of improper beliefs that caused the wrongdoing.

Siegfried understood that he would have to make all possible efforts to find this man, and to learn why the system that screened candidates for the Brotherhood had apparently failed. He was responsible for taking action to put the proper safeguards in place to protect 'the Mysteries'.

Would Siegfried encounter a man, more powerful than himself, drunk on temporal power and perhaps having awesome abilities in the inner planes? Such a man would soon come to a grievous end. The history of the Order had made it clear that those who put their abilities on display attract dangerous company. Many had been imprisoned, forced to carry out endless transmutations by political rulers, or by the heads of the

Church, to multiply their riches. Others were forced, under torture, to write manuscripts that divulged the secrets of alchemy.

Richard remembered the Professor explaining that many of the alchemical treatises were useless, written by genuine alchemists under extreme coercion or by people who wanted to sell books but knew nothing. Others still were produced under the guidance of the Church as disinformation, to discredit alchemy, and other paths that dared approach God without the priest as a necessary intermediary.

Richard and Melissa considered that Siegfried might find a man already at peace with himself, and at peace with the unfolding love and harmony of divine being, made possible by the immeasurable power of the Elixir of Life. Perhaps they would never know what happened to Herr Hoffman, and never know the fate of one who partook of the Philosopher's Stone.

Nearly it had been their privilege to know such; after the demonstration of a transmutation by the Professor, they were each to have been given small pieces of the Stone, and were to be shown the apparatus and processes that lead to the success.

They had been told that the method was that outlined by the adept Nicholas Flamel, and that it was in a rare manuscript, with an additional commentary by Flamel that would now be revealed only to the members of the highest grades of the Order, indicating the required steps in great detail.

These details were conveyed through codes or symbol systems of various sorts. They were to take the manuscript, and to make exact copies of it, down to the precise spacing of each letter on the page. While they would be shown the first part of the work by the Professor, the process of seeding the animated mercury would be withheld. The Professor had revealed, in somber tones, "This must come through your own efforts and contemplation. It can be revealed in no other way. The keys are qabalistic".

After the murder, Richard had agreed to make two copies of the manuscript, and to make two copies of the qabalistic diagram that they hoped would reveal the keys. The diagram was an ancient, water-stained parchment that they had found among a small cache of papers in a locked desk in the Professor's room. Melissa had agreed that they would take it with them.

Richard had been faithful to his promise, and had diligently made the copies. He had started as soon as they had settled in Austria, the process taking almost two months. This was not due to the length of the texts, for the qabalistic formulae were in the form of a single diagram, and the other, by Flamel, was twenty-two pages of text with illustrations facing the text. The first diagram, that of the so-called *tree of life*, was a highly complex arrangement of symbols, painted in now-faded pastel hues. In addition, there was ornately lettered Latin text interspersed with Hebrew letters covering the entire sheet. This had taken the first three weeks to copy. The remaining four weeks were required to make a facsimile of the Flamel text. Indeed, the moon had been new on the night that he had started, and once again new on the night that he finished.

The transformation in Richard was significant. He had learned more of qabala from this one drawing than from the three years of preparatory study that he had undergone in the work of the Order. Of course, those studies had prepared him to comprehend this rather tersely worded treatise, but still, the tree had come to life in his consciousness in a way that it had never done before. Now he understood qabala to be more than a mere intellectual creation; in fact the tree represented that which he had been told that it was – a map, or a glyph of Being and Creation itself.

The Professor had once told Richard that he had long ago found a 12th century document, a veritable treasure, which had been the product of some unfortunate Hebrew rabbi who had been forced to reveal certain keys to his captors. Apparently, a community of learned men had traveled to Spain and had kept alive, in the confines of their daily practice, certain symbolic representations of the universe that had been revealed to their priests during the period of captivity in Egypt. In time, their presence was looked upon with suspicion, and their material successes and seeming happiness and easiness envied. Their fortunes were seized and their books examined for evidence of a system of 'magic' that fueled their considerable affluence. One of them had apparently revealed, under circumstances that one can only imagine, certain keys to the practical qabala. While the author had intentionally distorted several things, the revelation of some of the keys was unique to this document and provided, when rectified though other works, practical keys to the alchemical work as well as to qabala.

Richard was convinced that the document he had taken after the Professor's death was either the original or a very old copy made from the original in the same manner he had just done.

The Flamel text had been done afterwards, so that the keys to the qabala would be fresh in his mind from the exhaustive task of copying it in the finest detail. The plan had born fruit, for on each page, in each sentence, Richard saw that the seeming nonsensical words, the words that were inserted to mask the truth, were unveiled and clearly revealed certain of the processes that the Professor had demonstrated to them.

Thus, by the time that the task of making the copies was completed, Richard had formulated a complete approach to the work. What remained was to test his theory though practice. He had wasted no time in starting, and had contacted Siegfried and others so that they might obtain samples of the starting material for the Great Work from various locations. As Siegfried was traveling extensively and had the means to do so, he provided the most numerous samples.

The matter was to be antimony ore, straight from the mine. Samples had arrived, month by month, and he had tested them to see if they would demonstrate the particular qualities that were described by Flamel. Two batches ultimately did so, one of them from Hungary, and another from Romania. The former was tremendously expensive, and proved to be no better than the Romanian ore. Just in case the source should become unavailable at a later date, he had had three hundred pounds of the ore delivered, and he secured it under a heavy tarpaulin outside the back entrance to the laboratory.

Then he had begun the processes, one step after the other. The signs of success for each step that Flamel openly communicated in the text did not appear in the matter, but those that he revealed in the commentary and in the hidden qabalistic keys did.

After what seemed an eternity, Richard had come to the end of the processes that had been, over a number of months, revealed by his mentor. The Professor had not alluded to these as being related to a single formula, but rather revealed these as unconnected experiments, designed 'to demonstrate certain little-understood principles'.

Now, he must work out the final sequences in the Work of making the Red Stone. It was a dangerous technique that he must now master, as delicate as the former processes were crude. No more would he sweat and blister beside the furnace. The fire would be less intense, but now there was another danger: Quicksilver – metallic mercury – was a deadly poison, and he had already filled his lungs with it!

Once when testing an apparatus that he thought might be able to contain the venomous fumes, the water used to contain the fumes had been sucked back into the glowing retort as it began to cool, and the whole thing had gone off like a bomb, choking fumes filling the room in an instant. Melissa led him to the carpenter's home, where she had recently helped the wife to deliver twins and watched him through the night. While he was not in immediate danger, Melissa recognized symptoms of poisoning: Richard could not concentrate, became angry when she would talk to him, in part because he was forgetting words that she had just said, and could not communicate. So odd, that Mercury was the mythological ruler of communications, the messenger of the gods. He seemed locked inside himself, not talking to his friends who let them stay until their cottage could be aired out. He was so moody! He had trouble sleeping, and when he did, he was being pulled out of his body, he would find himself in the astral realms. Even here, he was confused, angry, and fearful.

The next day, she returned to their home, and opened the windows and doors to air it out. Later, the walls, ceilings, and floors, and everything inside the house had to be wiped down. Fortunately the lab floor was stone, and could thoroughly be cleaned. This was a major setback to his work. Hard physical labor, special herbs to flush his system, and steam baths were part of the healing regimen that Melissa supervised. Richard responded quickly.

Concerned that there may be other mishaps, Melissa had insisted that Richard was to take no further risks with the equipment for distilling the animated mercury. They had a sizable inheritance, and he was to spare no expense in obtaining safe equipment. So, he had set about learning more about distilling the metal, and came up with a design for containing it. Melissa suggested a glass blower that had made equipment for her father, and he offered some useful design improvements. It worked perfectly, and as long as he managed the heat, and kept it working slowly, there was very little danger to them. Now, finally, he could begin to test his theory, to see if he could make the Red Stone.

Chapter 8

Thinking to get at once all the gold the goose could give, he killed it and opened it only to find - nothing.

- Aesop (620 BC - 560 BC), <u>The Goose with the Golden Eggs</u>

There was nothing about the two men that would attract attention. Careful planning allowed them to travel from country to country without appearing to be strangers.

They kept to themselves when they could, and they had need for little more than the necessities of transportation, food and lodging. The younger man was somewhat emaciated, but apparently in good health, and of a very pleasant nature. His companion dressed as an older man might, but was very limber and didn't tire from their extensive travels. They had been in India, Persia, Egypt, Morocco, Greece and Italy, and had, for the most part, sought company among the common people, deciding to avoid the areas that were most agreeable to European tourists. In each country, the older man introduced his younger companion to the most interesting people. Among the villages, and in the crowded communities built up around narrow winding streets and alleys, they had contacted representatives of numerous esoteric schools.

In India and Persia they had made contact with two branches of a small, very guarded sect of Zoroastrians. They were welcomed here after the older man had given particular passwords to these cautious men. In Egypt, a group of Gnostics were their hosts for several weeks, and were told of other groups operating in other lands. In Italy they had met with Templars, and there and also in Greece, a Pythagorean school in full operation had been discovered.

Henri was amazed by how readily the doors to the secret schools were opened to his companion. Though he was often in countries for the first time, Karl was able to immediately pick out in a village the family around which the school had its center, and to identify himself as a 'brother'. Henri had been of the Brotherhood too, but did not yet grasp the subtle means by which his companion made the required connections. It was true, however, that he was beginning to understand that the real communication was a psychic one, and that it was more in this way than through any outward sign that Karl made himself known.

The Professor once said, "In this lifetime, I have not been to Egypt or Morocco, and yet, I know these streets, these faces, these subtle symbols that indicate the portals to the various places which conceal the mysteries. When we first met with the Zoroastrians, we were asked, both of us, 'Why have you not come before? Your brothers and sisters have long sent their love and respect and hoped that we would meet with you again. Come and rest again among us, as you have for so many times before.'

"Do you understand that time changes very little for these schools? There is the fundamental vibration of the particular gnosis, the divinely revealed wisdom. To it come those who seek to kindle that flame which burns within them until it can no longer be contained. They wish to light the path, so that those of us who seek their companionship will find their very hearts to be the radiant beacons that lead back to the source of all".

Henri had been transformed by the journey. He knew not what his life to come would be; only that it was radically changed. All that was had been destroyed, had been purged and had flown away from the pure fire of the Stone. He had nearly killed the man that he most loved in order to have it, had nearly lost his soul in trade for mortal needs, to avoid a death that he no longer feared. His mind had been seriously shocked, in the first place by the revelations that came as his body was transformed. The rapid pace of travel to various countries had permitted him insufficient time to regain his balance. It was as though his companion had intentionally set out to keep him moving from place to place, to permit him to live life without expectation, without mundane goals, without becoming fixed in any particular place or time. How could he even hope to return home, where he was now sought as a murderer? Now he was exiled, with the man who did not die, and who may not yet die for a long time.

Chapter 9

*Go my sons, sell your lands, your houses, your
garments and your jewelry; burn up your books, buy
yourselves stout shoes, get away to the mountains and
the valleys, through the deserts, investigate the shores of
the sea and the deepest recesses of the earth. Be not
ashamed to learn by heart the astronomy and the
terrestrial philosophy of the peasants. In this way will
you arrive at a knowledge of things and their
properties.'*

-Petrus Severinus (Peder Sorensen), 1571

Melissa awoke with a start. She had been talking to her father! She was sitting on the bed, facing the table in the middle of the room, her feet firmly planted on the thick wool rug in front of the bed. It took her a moment to realize that she was just awakening from a deep sleep, and that she was, indeed, sitting upright. She felt vitalized, as though she had just finished a period of meditation. The clock struck the half-hour.

The clock was lighted by the silvery reflections of the moon, and at a glance she noted that it was now half-past two. There was no chance that she could fall asleep again. She wanted to get up and clean the house, or take a walk; she was so full of energy. Where was Richard? She sensed that he was in the laboratory, as he often was at this time, but there was no sound to indicate that he was still at work. Perhaps he had stepped out for a moment. Melissa sprung from the bed to go and look for him.

Richard opened his eyes, to find the candle fluttering, almost flashing off and on. The single chime of the old clock filled the front room with its sonorous voice. He sensed that there was no motion in the air, no draft to move the flame. It started coming back to him, the long visit he had had, the encouragement about the work he was doing in the laboratory, the patient touch of an old friend's hand. He had not felt that particular warmth, that closeness with a brother since...

Melissa burst into the room, her hair wild, and a huge smile on her face. Richard jumped as though he was a toy clown on a spring, and Melissa laughed. "I am not a spirit. Do I look quite that bad?" She brushed her hair back with her hands, and pursed her lips. "Were you asleep? I didn't hear you at work."

"I just woke up. You startled me!" he grumbled. "I was having a very nice dream. It was your Father, Missy. We had a long visit. I felt his hand on my shoulder. Is it possible that he is still in contact with us? Has he ever..."

"Apparently he has a lot to say to both of us, I woke up to find that I had been sitting on the bed talking to him. I had longed to hear his voice for these many months. I'm happy, Richard. He is all right. I know that, and I know we are not separate. He is with us. Right now though, I don't think I can sleep. And I'm too excited to talk. Are you sleepy, lover?"

She dropped the thin gown to the floor. Her breasts shone in the pale light reflecting through the room, her moist lips parted for a kiss. She felt herself in warm strong hands, felt the touch of the tip of his tongue between her lips, then, his lips and beard wandering down her front. She clasped him close, trying to push his entire body into hers. They made explosive love. In the silence that came after, they talked softly of their changing world, of their dreams, of their love for each other, and then made love again.

Over the next days, until the time that Adam and Mary returned, Richard rose early, often going with Melissa into the meadows, and found the shade of a tree, making his study here until time for lunch. He carried with him one book, a book of Ulstadius that the Professor had directed him to in the dream. He studied it, and made copious notes, until the sun was high, and the time for harvest was done.

They would eat bread and cheese together, and drink cool water from the brook. Richard talked about his ideas on how to complete the work, how they were to work together on the delicate seeding. Melissa showed him samples of the herbs she was harvesting. The borage was tall and its five-pointed stars of blue delighted them both. They cast a few flowers into the brook, and made wishes as the little blue constellations were swept away.

She always took a few pennies, some crystals, and other little gifts to bury beside the plants that she was to harvest. "It is an offering, a gift in exchange for their love and their life. It shows the plants that we do not use them without respect for their tender life. I pledge to them to use them to heal and to bring good cheer and gladness." She did the harvesting alone, but she would let him help her to carry the herbs to the drying shed, before the heat of the day took away their essences. Then, they were ready for their simple lunch. Afterwards, she would walk until late afternoon, when the shadows were growing long. He liked to watch her, and he could often catch sight of her light colored dress as she made her way across the meadows, following the brook at times, and other times crossing back and forth over the crest of the rolling hills.

One day she had taken him to another place. It had taken much of the morning to walk there. They came to an old bridge, its stone a rusty color. They walked across it, looking down at the swirling waters of the creek as it dropped several times across broad stones. The falls were not more than eight feet tall at any single place, but there the level of the creek dropped almost twenty feet in a short distance. It was absolutely beautiful. Melissa had mentioned 'going to the falls', but he had never imagined anything so wonderful.

"We are going up there, Richard. Come on!" She had pointed to a high cliff, more than one hundred feet above the creek. The path was steep, and they were going to have to ford the creek just at the crest of the falls. "It's easy. Just don't fall!" Melissa called back. She was already half way across the creek, her skirt tied in a knot to hold it above her knees.

Richard sat down on a dry stone. He took off his shoes and tied the strings together so that he could hang them around his neck, and carefully rolled up his pants legs and stuffed his socks in his pockets. By the time he was done, he could see Melissa standing on a rock on the other side, a full thirty yards from him. He started in. The rocks were slippery with green slime, and the water was icy cold, pressing against him with startling urgency. The sound of the falls was louder than he had expected. Step by step he made his way across, and finally Melissa extended her hand. She helped steady him as he stepped up onto the narrow rock shelf where she stood, holding to a thick root that was exposed in the soft dirt. Drat! There was no way he could put his shoes back on here!

Her feet were hardened from going without shoes, and he envied the way that she made it easily up the side of the cliff. She knew every branch, every shelf of rock, and she virtually slithered like a snake up the side of the limestone cliffs. Once she pointed out some unusual fossils, buried ages ago when this was the bottom of an ocean. He was able to find a large shelf of rock, wide enough for him to sit and quickly lace on his shoes. It was covered with loose pieces of crumbling soft stone, and he nearly slid off when he lifted his foot. He had nearly dropped the bottle he had brought for their lunch. This was not his element, and he wondered why he was risking his life on the side of some slab of rock.

"Come on, Richard! We are almost there. I want to show you something," came Melissa's voice from far above and to his right. He turned his head to look, being careful not to shift his weight too quickly. She was about fifteen feet above him, and as far to his right, leaning out from a clump of brush. She jerked her head back and started up again. He searched for a handhold and found one. He seemed to recall someone warning him that snakes like to sun themselves on warm ledges of rock. The crest of a cliff was not the place to discover napping serpents, he thought. After taking one more precarious step to a flat of rock that allowed for good footing, Richard saw that there was now an easy path before him, and soon walked up the path to where Melissa was sitting on a shelf of rock, leaning against a thick pine tree.

"Do you come up here often? This is dangerous, Melissa."

"Almost every week I take a walk up here. Look, Richard! Look." He carefully made his way out to her. He sat on ledge, smoothed by centuries of wind and rain. The thick bed of evergreen needles was soft, and the fragrance of the tree was lovely. The sun was still high in the sky, but there was little wind and the warmth was comforting. There, far below them was the series of falls, and upstream the gentle rapids foamed white. The bridge looked absolutely tiny, like a toy. He could see the chimney and the dark green roof of a small house that he had not seen from the bridge. There was wash hanging on the clothesline behind the house, wee specks of white and pastel making a strand of little pearls. Behind the house on a wide shelf of limestone that stretched along the rushing water was a small fire. Probably to burn trash, he thought. The thin wisp of smoke went straight up and far above the house before it dissipated.

The road wound around and between the hills, following the shape of the creek as it bowed around the base of their cliff. Beyond it laid the hills that led to their own tiny house. The green was so intense, like the green that appears after a rain, only with hints of gold from the intense sun. The sky was perfect! He sighed deeply.

"So?"

"It is lovely, I can see why you come here", said Richard. He was relaxed, and yet stimulated from the long morning walk and the strenuous climb. They shared a bottle of cider, some cheese and herbal bread. As they ate, they watched little lizards sunning on the ledges of rock.

Melissa turned and walked in a crouch out to the path, where she stood up and brushed off her skirt. "Let's go, I want to show you some things, so we can get back home before it gets too dark".

They spent the rest of the afternoon walking. The variety of flowers and animals amazed Richard. There were tiny twittering birds, blue with an orange breast, flying in pairs, and bright yellow ones as showy as any canary. They heard the sounds of woodpeckers drilling for food, and the scolding of squirrels.

Melissa had stopped to point out the droppings of a deer when they were crossing one of the several old stone fences. Later they had seen a doe and her fauns, and had watched them for several minutes before they bounded out of sight into the deep woods. For a time, a vulture and a large golden hawk soared lazily in the sky.

They had found a salamander, too. This particularly fascinated Richard, as the salamander was an alchemical symbol. They had noticed a red fox, standing by a rotting log that had turned rust red in color. It was as though the log and animal were made out of the same magnificent ochre. The fox stood motionless for a moment, then turned and immediately ran into the brush. Melissa took up a large stick and had easily turned over a section of the log.

The salamander was nearly as long as Melissa's foot, its skin as black as polished coal, with brilliant spots of orange and red. Richard touched it and found that it was somewhat agreeable to his inspection.

"I don't think this one would live in a fire for long," he laughed, recalling the alchemical myth.

Melissa smiled and asked, "The rotting of the tree is a slow fire isn't it? Rotting burns all things given enough time."

They put the shiny newt back into its hiding place, taking care to replace things just as they had been.

The plants had been as varied as the animals. There were stands of poplar, elm, oak and pine. Motherwort, chamomile, wild roses, yarrow and heal-all were plentiful and grew vigorously. There were meadows of tall grass that made ghost-like whispering sounds at the slightest breeze, and beyond them were fruit trees, and the ruins of an old house. Perhaps some of the herbs had been first brought here for a garden and had escaped into the verdant paradise that stretched all around them.

They had picked handfuls of berries and had sat on the old stone foundations like two children at a tea party, eating and laughing. By the time that they had finished exploring the old ruins, and had delighted in touching the thick, cool mosses and reading the old medicine bottles that littered what had been the back of the house, they noticed that it was now decidedly cooler. And darker! The sun was nearly down, and they were several miles from the cliffs. They would have to go down the cliffs in the dark!

They scrambled back across the fields, and managed to find the paths easily in the dimming light. They snaked their way back through the tangles of barbed wire, and were soon back at the place where Richard had first looked out at the valley. The west was a dim red orange, with delicate low clouds of violet blue. They stood transfixed as the top of the shimmering disk poked its head back under the earth. Above, they saw the twinkle of Venus and Saturn, against a purplish velvet sky.

There was a light in the window at the little cottage by the bridge. "We'd better get going, if we are not going to spend the night here," Melissa said, trying to sound as though it was a joke.

"Yeah, I guess we'd better. Ladies first."

Melissa knew the way well, and they came down the steep cliff with little trouble. At times, she had reached up to help Richard find the proper foothold in the dark. As they got closer to the base of the hill, they could hear the rushing of the creek, and the calls of the whip-poor-will. They walked across the edge of the waterfall, and then home, across the hills. There had been no moon, and yet the sky was so clear and bright that the stars cast shadows at their feet. They had seen and heard the ripping sound of a large shooting star, looking at the sky together, then at each other. The magic was perfect.

Chapter 10

"Friendship is a single soul dwelling in two bodies."
  - Aristotle

Richard had been glad to return to his work. From the first of August until the middle of the month, he had found it almost too hot to work in the laboratory. He had been meditating, keeping notes regarding dreams and other inspirations about seeding the Philosopher's Mercury. He had decided to use calx of gold as the seed – gold would be divided into atoms by some Philosopher's Mercury, and forcefully distilled with added sea salt to carry away all but the gold, then reduced to a golden brown powder. This was the so-called 'rich man's path'. It was, after all, the Royal Art.

The fields beyond their home were beginning to beckon to him. Also, he sensed a dramatic change in Melissa, and wanted to share in it. She had become increasingly playful and youthful again. The beauty of Nature had restored and renovated her.

She had confided to Richard that she had felt her Father's presence several times in recent weeks, and that while she could not always remember all of the conversations, that she always felt at peace, and felt the comfort once again of having his support and his love.

Richard told her, at first reluctantly, and then eagerly, "I have also had continued contact with your father. It is when I am in a dream state, apparently, and in the very clear sort of dreams, the kind of dreams in which you and I sometimes meet. It is as though he is creating most of the dream contents, which makes it very different. I realize that some of it is my doing; I can recognize that I have full volition, but it is in scenes that are not familiar to me. One night during my dreams I had to chase him down winding alleys, past beggars, street vendors, and old people sitting in their doorways. It was broad daylight, and he was very decidedly trying to elude me. He lost me for a minute when I came around a turn and ran into a group of playing children.

"Quite by intuition, I saw a man sitting in front of his shop, mending a brass urn. There were all of these ornate bowls and other brass pieces stacked around the narrow doorway to the shop. I just pushed my way past him and then past the curtain hanging in the very back of the shop. He was there with a group of men, all of them with very long beards. They looked at me, startled. He smiled, and took me by the arm, and led me out of the room, into the front part of the shop. We talked about the process that I am currently working on in the lab. He was enjoying the effect that the strange situation was having on me. He did nothing to lessen my confusion, but had me sit by him at the rude fireplace that had been used to cook the midday meal. There was an older woman there, and two younger girls, but they hid their faces, and stayed as distant from us as the small quarters would permit.

"We sat for a time, and he confirmed to me that I had deciphered a particular process for seeding the matter to obtain the Red Stone. He referred to three distinct texts and told me at length how each of them hinted at the real process. It was simple, if you understood what was being done; otherwise, each process seemed a different approach. I recall everything he said, Melissa, and it is something that I had not even suspected before. It will work!"

Melissa had not taken her eyes from Richard the entire time he spoke. She nodded to acknowledge his explanation, then said, "Richard, when Father and I talk, it is like old times; he gives me instructions for specific exercises, how to use my psychic centers to strengthen my attunement, how to use specific herbs to assist in the process. That reminds me, do you have any sundew? It doesn't grow well here – there are no really good marshy lands nearby."

He stammered, started to say something and thought better of it, and then went out to the front of the house and sat in the shade, his back against the house.

Melissa followed him, asking, "Richard, what is it?"

"Last night, when your father and I met again, he showed me a handful of a red-brown herb and dropped it onto the ground. It started to writhe like little worms, and then it began to sprout into little tree-like things, green and glistening with tiny drops of dew.

He said it was *ros solis* and that it was 'in *Malkuth*, with all of the rays'. That is sundew, isn't it, Missy? On the tree of qabala, *Malkuth* is the realm at the very bottom of the tree which corresponds to our physical level of reality where the emanations of all the planetary energies are collected. He once told me that antimony is unique among the metals because it too is related to *Malkuth*; this makes it a key for the work of the Philosopher's Stone. He never mentioned that there was a plant with these properties."

"*Ros solis* is an old Latin name for the sundew plant. Did Father say where to find it?"

"In the dream, as he spoke this, I was at the same time picturing you and me in the banks along the creek, just behind the little house by the red bridge that we went to. Maybe it is there."

"Thank you, Papa! I've never looked there, because when I go there, I visit with the woman who lives there. Tomorrow I will look. It is like Father has never really left us, isn't it, Richard?"

"Missy, he seems more alive than anyone – just different. It makes me think of the poem: *'Do not stand at my grave and weep; I am not there, I do not sleep'*."

Melissa made her trip to look for the sundew the next morning. The old woman who lived by the creek indeed knew where to find the 'fly catchers' as she called them. There was a marshy bog that was full of the insect-eating plant, and as the woman had no use for them, Melissa could take what she needed. She had taken the old woman two loaves of homemade bread and a jar of berry jam. Melissa returned the next afternoon with oil distilled from egg yolks to help soften the hard crusts of skin that protruded from the old woman's hands and face.

Annie was a proud old woman, quite hard of hearing, and Melissa found it necessary to shout when she wanted to speak to her. Most of the time, it was quite unnecessary, as Annie 'knew' what the young woman thought. They spent many hours together after that, for Melissa found her company very pleasant, and the old woman thoroughly enjoyed the occasional visits. They laughed like sisters.

For as long as she and Richard had lived in the area, Melissa had walked by the tiny house at least once a week when checking on her herbs. She had seen the old woman only a few times. Annie was always wearing an old-fashioned sunbonnet, faded to a delicate robin's egg blue with a repeating pattern of white flowers. Her face was like leather, tanned by the sun and wind. Her hands were strong from working her garden and repairing the house and outbuildings. She had three goats for company and for the sweet milk.

She had showed Melissa how to make a blend of valerian root and 'bicarbonate' in goat's milk, which made a very relaxing potion to assure a restful and regenerating sleep. Melissa shared with her the locations of the various healing herbs growing along her property and brought her plenty of seed and dried plants.

In exchange, Annie patiently explained about the herbal lore of her peoples; she was half Romanian gypsy, half Armenian. Her wisdom concerning both diagnosis and healing was seemingly boundless, and yet she seemed excited to share in Melissa's knowledge as well. She had no living children, and was content to live a contemplative life, supporting herself from her garden, storing the bounties of the warm months in the cellar for the hard winter months. She also managed to cut enough wood to get through a winter without being dependent on anyone's help. Annie was as independent as they came. Her deafness seldom proved to be a liability, for she seldom had visitors, seldom left her property.

She had turned down Melissa's invitation to come for Sunday dinner, in fact, had turned down several of them, but had told Melissa, "You bring your man here. I'll cook for you." Melissa had hesitated, fearful that the woman might serve them food that she would need for herself during the coming winter.

One Sunday, Melissa had 'felt funny' about Annie and had asked Richard to get dressed and go with her to see the old woman.

"Finally," he had teased, "I get to meet the goat lady that you've told me about. Most of those old women use a cat as a familiar... they are generally easier to get along with than goats. Not as good to eat, however."

"Richard! Stop it!" Melissa scolded, whipping a shawl over her shoulders with one hand and slapping his arm with the other. "We need to get started."

As they came around the final bend before the road looped back across the bridge, Melissa had been relieved to see that there was a plume of smoke rising from the chimney. "She must be all right Richard. I felt so queer about her though; I thought of her before I awoke, as though it was urgent that we come".

Annie had welcomed them at the front door, her dark eyes twinkling like black diamonds. She had motioned them into the house, and without a word walked in behind them and closed the door against the cool Autumn wind. "There's a small fire to warm our bones before we partake," she said.

Melissa and Richard stood in stunned silence. The table was spread with bowls and baskets heaped with food. The smells were absolutely enticing. "Who's coming to eat?" Melissa yelled to the old woman.

"I invited some herb woman and an alchemist. They are due about now," she cackled.

After prayer, holding hands around the table, Melissa was more herself, realizing that she had been wrong to assume that Annie had inadequate provisions. The food was delightful to the eye and nose.

"This looks wonderful, Annie, and I'm glad that Missy thought to bring me along," Richard had said as he sat by Annie.

"The invitation was clear enough, I think," came the old woman's response.

Richard hesitated for a moment when Annie passed him a fragrant stew. "It's a rabbit that fattened itself off my garden all year, not one of my prize goats, if that is what you are worried about. I shot him this morning."

They feasted on wild greens, potatoes and cheese, and a spicy tomato and pepper dish. "Everything here I either shot or plucked out of the ground. Or churned. Except for this jam that you brought me, Missy. God is good to us, children, and I am pleased to share what I have received through His generosity. Melissa has been so good to me, and has been welcome company for an old woman".

After they had eaten, they sat beside the fire. Richard had obviously taken to Annie, for he talked rather openly about his work in alchemy, which was not his custom. He had kept his responses rather brief, since he had to yell, and he was not used to straining his voice. Once or twice he had been trying to think how to explain something to her that was difficult to tell in a few words. As he did so, he felt a twinkling sensation in the center of his forehead, and looked up to see her intent look, and open smile. Finally, he understood.

"Are you hearing me now?" he asked silently, directing the words mentally to her forehead.

"You don't have to shout," came the reply. "Unless you just like to!" she cried out, slapping her thighs and laughing until her eyes watered.

Richard laughed, and turned to his wife, "Melissa, why didn't you tell me that Annie..."

"I just forgot to mention it Richard, I just take it for granted that you can read my thoughts and I can read hers. It just seemed like a little thing".

"Oh hell. I know where you got the idea about the goat stew," suddenly realizing that his new friend Annie had quite a sense of humor.

"Well, it didn't bother me any, but I'm not so sure about the goats." Annie moved her chair toward the couple, and put her hands on theirs. "I have a few things to tell you. I know that things have been troublesome for you. Not so much lately, but before. Everything is well, and is as it should be. The man that you think is a murderer is innocent. Tell your friend, I don't know his name, the tall one."

"Siegfried," Richard answered.

"Tell him to stop looking. The man is not to be found. He didn't hurt anyone. He needs to disappear for a time before he comes back. He will not look as he did before, but you will know him."

"If you know all of this, Annie, then who killed my father? If you are going to take the only logical suspect away from us by maintaining that he is innocent, then tell me who has done this to us!" Richard pulled his hands away from Annie's and put his arms around his wife, pulling her close.

"Your father killed himself, in a way. It was the only way for him to escape. He had begun to change once he made the Red Stone. He realized what was happening to his body and his mind, and he had to leave everyone he knew. He is alive now, and he is with the man you seek. They are now both changed."

"Annie, if this is not true, then I beg you to stop!" Melissa's eyes filled with tears. "This is hard for me. I cannot bear it, even from you, Annie."

"Annie is telling the truth, Melissa. I know it," proclaimed Richard, as he turned to the old woman, searching her mind. He felt peace when he connected with this woman, as though all things were written on leaves of purest gold, delicate as silk. He could sense places far away, and felt as though he wanted to touch her.

"Take my hands, dear ones," she spoke. "Let me show you what has been, and what is".

Annie and Richard were back in the house where they had first met. The smells of the laboratory that mingled with rich old incenses and the fragrance of a spotlessly clean home surrounded them. They were on the porch at the back of the house, and the old shed was as it had been. They saw the Professor and the man who they had supposed to be his murderer at work in the shed. They heard the voices of the Professor and Herr Hoffman.

"We must work quickly. Here, this is going to be a bit messy, but it is the only way." The Professor pushed a little bundle into the other man's hands. "He has no teeth to speak of. Try to get as many of these into his jaws as you can. The identification must be positive."

They watched as Herr Hoffman sat the corpse upright and tried to open his mouth. He vomited.

"Please hurry. They are waiting," urged the Professor. Together, they had worked, one prying the mouth open and the other pushing the teeth into the bloodless gums. The Professor helped to place the body on his back, and then reached for a knife, making a deep stab into the abdomen, and then slashed across. Together, the two turned the stolen medical cadaver face down.

"The facial features will not matter. He is close enough, I guess, in build. We have to make sure that we don't blow ourselves up in starting the fire. Here. Help me open these sacks". They tore open bags of niter and dumped the powerful oxidizer on the floor, and poured most of the oil from the lantern over it. The Professor directed the other man, who took a bottle of acid and poured it in the floor, making certain to douse the man's face where it pressed against the floor.

"This is ghoulish, Karl. The smell!" He vomited again.

"Here, this is the last of it," grunted the Professor. He had poured fully five liters of alcohol on the floor, and then tossed a shovel full of sulphur over it.

The Professor and his assistant then did as rehearsed. The Professor left the shed and took up his place near the door. Hoffman banged the flat side of a coal shovel against the inside shed wall nearest the house to attract attention. The Professor shouted, "You bastard! Leave me! I have guests here. They will hear you! Leave now, Hoffman!"

Hoffman whispered, "She is at the back of the house now, Karl." The Professor nodded, and Hoffman stepped back from the shed, now in plain sight of Melissa, and screamed, "You abandoned me to die. It is wrong, Karl. You are wrong! I am going to..."

Richard and Melissa watched the vision unfold, as Hoffman threw the lantern into the shed. There was a hot geyser of flame, moist and blue. "Sweet Jesus!" Hoffman screamed, and then ran into the bushes at the end of the property, where the Professor waited. "You nearly killed me, with that fire, Karl! Lieber Gott!"

The Professor smiled at Hoffman. "We are even, now! We must leave at once! Get going. We will be out of the country by morning. Here, you must take this medicine now. It will make you very ill, and will make you very dull. It is necessary that we keep others from searching for your mind, because they can find us out".

"Are the effects..."

"Permanent? No. In a few days the elixir that you have taken earlier this evening will begin its work in earnest, and you will be healed. Otherwise, yes, your mind would be destroyed, I fear. Please, we must go now, Hoffman."

The smell had been hideous, the fire a devouring dragon. Richard and Melissa watched as Siegfried came to the shed, and heard the windows shatter and drop into the inferno. The wind that whipped through the shed now had transformed the little building into a blast furnace. The fumes were choking. Siegfried dropped to his knees and pressed his face against the earth. The figure of a man lay in the floor, dark and motionless, disappearing as the roof beams collapsed, the noise all but drowning out the cry of a man whose heart was being ripped from his chest. "Karl! My brother!"

Richard and Melissa now witnessed a number of rapidly unfolding scenes. At first they saw the two men in an abandoned office at the university, where they had spent the night. Just before dawn, they were moving again, this time to the train station. In the next scene, the two men watched the scenery change from a private car on the train. They ate and slept, but seldom spoke. The man with the Professor became ill and stayed in his compartment for two days. When he emerged, he looked pink, wrinkled, like an infant. He looked vulnerable and new, like an insect just emerged from its transparent chrysalis. In his former illness he looked like a man who was sick and tired from the effort of living. Now he looked shiny, as though his veins were filled with liquid gold, heavy and luminescent. He appeared as though he was just now beginning to realize his strength, as if he now could accomplish any task, could champion any cause. His eyes were liquid pools of light, as were those of his companion. The Professor looked like a mature specimen of whatever it was; the other was a new hatchling.

The pair did not, to the casual observer, appear particularly different from their companions on the train. The one with pink flesh appeared as many whose skin is so fair that they seldom venture out into the glaring sun. Yet there was a cast of gold to their skins. In the case of the elder man, it appeared as if he had been lightly dusted with minute flecks of gold. Richard and Melissa could see the auras of the men, could see the shifting violet-white, tinged with golden flares that emanated from their bodies. They observed how others would look at the men for a moment, and then look away and back again, as though they were sensing something that their eyes could not quite see. The men mostly ate fruits and light courses of vegetables. Once, the younger man, delighted to be feeling stronger once again ordered a meal of cheese soup, followed by a rich meat dish in a heavy sauce. He was able only to pick at his meal, to eat some bread and the salad. The wine that he ordered went almost untouched. "You will find that everything is changed. Your thoughts will become as light as feathers, your cares little, and your patience endless. Your appetite for life will be increased beyond your former capacity, but this too will be different. You will not care for rich food and drink, and you will find that you can draw sustenance out of the thin air. Your vision will dance with new images, of new worlds, and yet you will be fully a master in this world. What did you dream of last night?"

"There was a strange land with the largest trees, whose tops could not be seen, and outrageously big flowers. I was taken to a place by a waterfalls that had many animals, some few of which I could recognize. There was an incredible amount of light – the sun was so bright that all was lit up from the inside – each stone and flower, each tree shone with its own interior light. The sky was so bright that you could see no details, only light. There were large animals flying through the air, as though they were swimming in it. It was totally unlike life here, yet it was absolutely real to me. I realized suddenly that all of my teeth were gone. It was then that I looked down at myself and saw that the intense light had set me aflame. I was burning, and yet it was not painful. It was actually pleasant. The impurities were being purged; they had been burned right out of me.

"Then, these men, I think there were six of them, took me with them to a castle. It had a long hallway that was totally filled with mirrors, and then the great room had the richest colored tapestries and rugs, and flags and banners on the walls. The banners all displayed the golden crown, surmounting a *fleur d'leis*. We stood silently for a time in the center of the great room, and then the ceiling opened up, the windows opened, and light poured in from all sides. The castle, the men and I were all gone; there was only a feeling of perfect peace, of perfect power, of pure consciousness.

"I had forgotten all about this dream! It was beautiful!" The man pushed away his dishes, and sat upright, hands flat on the table. "What does it mean?"

The Professor replied, "It has certain peculiar symbols that are absolutely consistent with what I have experienced. It has to do with an initiatic process – the castle is the temple, and the light that abounded has to do with the level that you are on. It is that of *Tiphereth*, a level shown on the Tree of Life of qabala as being on the central pillar, and associated with the Sun, with Apollo. This level brings the ability to heal at a distance or with the touch, and to have a clear vision of the interior worlds, including gifts of prophecy. The loss of teeth had taken place previously, and you noticed the burning of your body, but it had begun previously. These are symbolic that you had already progressed through the purification by the four elements, which culminates with the purification by fire. *Shin*, the Hebrew letter, as written represents a molar, a tooth, as well as tongues of fire. The initiation that you experienced is that of the Christic world, we might say. There will be more revealed to you in time. Do not rush it; it will come of its own accord."

Richard and Melissa, sitting in the home of an old woman by the red bridge observed the two men at first in Egypt, now in Morocco, then Algiers, and now in India, and Tibet. Each time that they saw the pair, the younger looked stronger and increasingly like the older man. Soon they appeared as though they were brothers by birth. They were always seen together, their auras bonded as though they were of one body.

AFTERWORD

The first pages of *The Portal* came quickly, during a brief lull at my office in 1994; I happened to recall a 'waking dream' I had experienced for a brief moment while relaxing in front of a friend's fireplace roughly a decade before. A memory from a past life? I was open to such an experience, but as I have a scientific mindset, I suspended my need to explain the momentary vision with such a label. All that the experience left for my conscious mind was a bit of residue – the image of a man working in the shadows of an alchemical furnace, "flapping around like a crow". I started typing, as though to take the image that I had and to explore it, to see where it would take me.

My wife Sue read the few pages I had typed, and then asked, "What happens next?" She was pleased to read the pages I would hand her when I came home from work, and I was curious what she would think about them. Quickly, the characters developed momentum. The story unfolded with little effort, within some few weeks, as I recall, the story was completed.

While I have been an avid reader since childhood, I had never been inclined to write fiction, and had given little thought to the craft of writing. The first real upset to this happily flowing process was trying to figure out what real novelists do, how they pace stories, decide what to leave out, and so on. And so a story that was written in 1995 has not been told until now. Don't get me wrong; I don't think for a moment that the world has been a poorer place because of that. However, it does interest me to see how self-consciousness and 'technique' can inhibit creativity.

Perhaps some readers wonder why someone would choose to write about alchemy, esoteric orders, and so on. It was certainly not prompted by a commercial interest, or, in fact, by an interest in writing a novel at all. *The Portal* represents some *bouillabaisse* of the imagination, with veiled personal experiences, and snippets of historical fact and legend that has emerged from my mind in a somewhat coherent manner.

I grew up in the era of the Sputnik, and was raised in the church. It seemed natural to me to that things should all fit together. I had a microscope, a telescope, and a chemical lab as a youth, and a family that encouraged me to learn. At church I heard about 'atheism', which made little sense to me at that tender age, as I felt that the wonders of creation were in front of our eyes continually, and that the harmony, order and rhythm apparent in Nature hinted at the presence of the Creator. I read incessantly, particularly at the borderland of science and religion, where many references to alchemy, and consequently to the enigmatic Rosicrucians appeared as signposts.

Physical laboratory alchemy plays a large role in this book. For those few who find such an arcane study of interest, I will say that it has been my great pleasure to know and to study with a number of generous souls, among them are Jean Dubuis, Frater Albertus, "Artofferus", George Fenzke, and Jack Glass.

Some readers may be, as I was, drawn to the study of alchemy, qabala or the Western esoteric path; I suggest that they consider the other publications of Triad Publishing, listed in this book, which offer practical and graded studies of these subjects, which are unique for their clarity and completeness.

My friend, Mark Stavish, author of <u>The Path of Alchemy - Energetic Healing and the World of</u>

Natural Magic and Kabbalah for Health and Wellness, offered many suggestions which have made the book more accessible to a general audience, and shared his insights regarding promotion and marketing. I very much appreciate his contribution.

My friend Lonnie Mack, long one of my favorite musicians and songwriters, read an earlier draft of *The Portal* and encouraged me to publish it.

My nephew, Stephen Bradley, an accomplished artist in many styles and media, recently ventured into publishing, and blazed a trail for me to follow. Thanks!

My sister, Eleanor Fryman Wilson, one of my earliest co-conspirators, encouraged me to observe Nature, and helped me to understand that not all of Nature is visible. We were fortunate to grow up in Kentucky, a land still beautiful and sacred.

My children, Jim, Mary, Katie, and Jon helped to turn me into a real adult, I hope that I can repay them by helping keep them child like.

Also available from

Triad Publishing
P.O. Box 116
Winfield, IL 60190 USA
www.triad-publishing.com

New in 2007:

<u>The Experience of Eternity</u>: This long-anticipated treatise was announced by Mr. Jean Dubuis, a respected French alchemist and scientist, more than a decade ago. The author presents an experimental method designed to lead one towards an interior experience of very high level, named here the *Great Experience*, the *Contact on Eternity* or the *Experience of the Point*. This unique method was designed to dispense with elaborate ritual, and the risk and expense of an alchemical laboratory, so that this important evolutionary path would be accessible to more persons. 175 pages; approximately 60,000 words with 37 illustrations and tables.

"Jean Dubuis' long awaited treatise, <u>The Experience of Eternity</u> may be the single most important esoteric document of the 21st Century. Densely written with 32 illustrations and diagrams, Dubuis presents classical esotericism, alchemy, qabala, and natural magic in a form that allows each person to undertake the road of interior initiation without need of a guru, master, or teacher. Extensive and detailed discussion of the creation of the universe, our place in it, and reason for being are all presented in clear and concise language. Methods given utilize the most nominal tools easily available locally or via the Internet. Among some of the topics addressed are man's inner structures, how to harmonize them, the role of visualization, dream symbols and their use, astrological timing for specific experiences, and how to anchor our inner work into our daily life. Be careful though, once read, and if successful, you may find yourself following the author's advice, pinched from the Polish alchemist Sendivogius, 'Now burn all your books, including mine'." – Mark Stavish, author of <u>The Path of Alchemy - Energetic Healing and the World of Natural Magic</u> and <u>Kabbalah for Health and Wellness</u>.

Also available from **Triad Publishing**

The Philosophers of Nature teachings: An association in France, Les Philosophes des la Nature (L.P.N.) developed a series of courses for their members, related to alchemy, qabala and Western esotericism. These courses were translated to English and distributed by the Philosophers of Nature (P.O.N.). By the year 2000, both organizations had been closed by their respective boards of directors. These English-language courses are available exclusively from Triad Publishing:

<u>**Fundamentals of Esoteric Knowledge**</u>: This 12 lesson course provides the background and overview needed to understand precisely the materials in the <u>Spagyrics</u>, <u>Mineral Alchemy</u> and <u>Qabala</u> courses. It is also an exceptional course on its own. The objective is to assist the student in becoming aware of the Path of Return and its significance. Provided exercises assist in contact with one's Inner Master.

<u>**Spagyrics**</u> is a 2-volume, 48-lesson course which details the preparation and uses of herbal elixirs, particularly the seven planetary elixirs used to rebalance the spiritual centers in the human body, the processes followed to obtain the vegetable stone (Opus Minor), the method for extracting the universal seed from rain water, and similar processes. Theoretical, practical and philosophical aspects of spagyrics are developed in the course materials. Theory on philosophical mercury and the alkahests is also given.

<u>**Mineral Alchemy**</u> is an 84 lesson course in 4 volumes, which builds on the information given in the <u>Spagyrics</u> course. The focus is on practical work in the mineral and metallic realm: preparation of menstruums, different paths for making animated mercury, separation of the three essentials, and related works. Among those whose methods are considered in this course are: Flamel, Philalethes, Newton, Von Bernus, Frater Albertus, Weidenfeld, Becker, Glaser, Basil Valentine, Hollandus, Paracelsus, and many others. Laboratory equipment required for the metallic work can be substantial, so alternatives to reduce costs are described where possible.

The practice of spagyrics and alchemy brings about an intimate knowledge of visible Nature, and its invisible energies – life and consciousness. This knowledge allows one to transmute themselves, to regenerate themselves, to attain Inner Initiation. Only then is the path of physical transmutation open to the initiate.

Qabala, is a 3-volume, 72-lesson course. The material is largely practical instruction, and differs from most information found in popular books on the subject. This course is rather concentrated and does require significant work; however, it provides teachings that are often spread out over a period of thirty or more years.

In addition, Triad Publishing offers videos of seminars held by the Philosophers of Nature, with instruction by Jean Dubuis and others, and volumes of newsletters of the association are available.

All English language courses
$199

Breinigsville, PA USA
10 November 2010
249134BV00001B/57/A